SPEAKING OF WORK
A Story of Love, Suspense and Paperclips

Jonathan Ames

-

Lee Child

-

Billy Collins

-

Sloane Crosley

-

Joshua Ferris

-

Jonathan Safran Foer

-

Roxane Gay

-

Valeria Luiselli

-

Alain Mabanckou

-

Aimee Mann & Jonathan Coulton

-

Joyce Carol Oates

-

Gary Shteyngart

Cover Design by Chip Kidd

SPEAKING OF

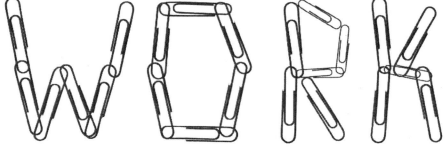

A Story of Love, Suspense and Paperclips

BERNARD SCHWARTZ
EDITOR

SLOANE CROSLEY
CREATIVE EDITOR

Xerox Corporation

Xerox Corporation
201 Merritt 7
Norwalk, CT 06851

Published globally by Xerox in 2017 as part of Project: SET THE PAGE FREE.

Xerox®, Xerox and Design®, ConnectKey®, DocuShare®, iGen4®, VersaLink®, Xerox Nuvera® and FreeFlow® are trademarks of Xerox Corporation in the United States and/or other countries. XMPie® is a registered trademark of XMPie, Inc. 10/2017

Printed in the United States of America.

Cover printed on a Xerox® iGen4® Press with Matte Dry Ink using a FreeFlow® Print Server.

Text printed on a Xerox Nuvera® 144 EA Production System using a FreeFlow® Print Server.

ISBN 978-0-692-93131-8

eBook ISBN 978-0-692-93132-5

To everyone, anywhere, who works.

CONTENTS

INTRODUCTION

—

Sloane Crosley

The thing most people don't consider about the cavemen is just how many of them worked in offices. Not all the cavemen, of course. Some were freelance boar hunters and berry gatherers, or else they whittled clubs with names like The Lady Sleeper 3000™. But the rest of the cave people woke up every morning, commuted to a different part of the cave, and got to work on a task for which they expected to be rewarded. History has been woefully negligent of these people. Who do you think sorted the sticks and organized the animal teeth? Who do you think saw reindeer trotting across the south of France and instead of thinking, "Oh good, food," thought, "Oh good, visual aids!" The planet's first office workers, that's who. The human imperative to produce on a regular basis—to excel and be of value—is a lot older than we tend to think it is. Which means that whatever you do for a living, it's probably closer to the world's oldest profession than what you have long assumed to be "the world's oldest profession." Probably.

Thousands of years later, it may be harder to achieve success in the modern world (a couple of loin cloths do not a fashion line make), but humans want more or less what we've always wanted—to find our role in life's cave. It's the workplace itself that's evolved. It's the workplace itself that's constantly in flux. And it is the workplace itself that's the focus of the eleven stories in this book. Here, some of today's most talented authors (and two singer-songwriters) come together in a kind of virtual office to ask themselves the same question: what does it mean to get to work *now*? As it would be in real life, each author has decorated his or her office differently. Some have used fiction, some autobiography, some poetry. But each story shares a thematic wall with the next. Organized in connected clusters, this book explores contemporary issues of mentorship, creation, competition, and even boredom.

These tales take place on street corners and in classrooms, in parking lots and Genius Bars. And because this virtual office is occupied by writers, who are rarely in danger of *under*thinking an issue, there's also plenty of nostalgia, of longing for the days of warm photocopies and nubby carpeting. And they're not alone. Open up the suite of office emojis on your phone and you'll find a floppy disk, a fountain pen, a push-button phone, and a Rolodex. This is because, while we weren't looking, the taste of burnt coffee and the sound of a fax machine jamming merged with our schema of the world. Time curled around the mundane and made it meaningful.

Which brings us back to our friends, the cavemen. While they may have had a sense of creating something great in the moment—an especially well-stretched animal hide, say—they surely did not believe that one day their descendants would walk through dark caverns to admire their handiwork. How could they have known? And how can we know what pieces of the modern workplace will stand the test of time? I suspect the vocational legacy we leave behind will be less about artifacts and more about the array of worlds on display in the narratives you're about to read. About how we got to work, about how we balanced passion with obligation and creativity with structure. Here is the modern workplace as it lives now, in twelve different imaginations. So please, come on in. The meeting's just down the hall in the conference room. They can't start without you.

IN THE BEGINNING

–

Sloane Crosley

t's hard not to have affection for our first jobs, the more ill-suited and miserable the better. Probably because learning who you're not is just as informative as learning who you are. I, for one, was an abominable assistant. I worked at a literary agency where I managed to make countless tiny mistakes that had impressive ripple effects. And yet I still get moony thinking about the thirteen and a half (who's counting?) months I spent as the worst assistant of my generation. This is because of what I got out of it—a new career direction and, eventually, a piece of writing based on it. Both well worth the price of admission. I'm happy to report that the story and the essay that kick off this book prove I'm in excellent company.

The narrator of Joshua Ferris's "Hedges & Balk" seems like an unlikely candidate for any sort of day job. He reads Faulkner, was "reared on Fugazi and Black Flag, the single-shooter games in cineplexes, and everything on offer at Taco Bell," but he finds himself manning the phones as a temp for a communications firm, the gateway to corporate America. He is, admittedly, "at odds with the target audience."

It's this contrast that gives the story its texture and energy—his day job itself serves as a kind of straight man to a life of all-nighters and pop-up parties, of free-spirited artist friends, some who get their due and some who never do. It's a poignant reflection on the contrasts between office life and nightlife, between making art and starting a career. Without the florescent lights of his days, the neon of his nights wouldn't burn as bright.

Meanwhile, in Gary Shteyngart's "Office Envy," he, too, finds himself out of place in his first job. Here the soundtrack is less Fugazi, more funhouse. He still longs for the camaraderie of the workplace, of the structure and socialization that eludes a fulltime writer. This is true even though, when he did have "real" jobs, he was "terribly incompetent at them." But these were his formative experiences. Furthermore, anyone who's ever been an assistant or an intern or a temp with artistic aspirations will relate to this sentiment: "We shared common goals of not wanting to do much, while also fully believing that we were better than the tasks assigned to us." And to think, millennials are credited with inventing creative laziness and casual insurgency. Please. Bow down, kiddos! The writers in this book have been figuring out how to take two-hour lunches since before there were screens in your pockets.

Chapter 1

HEDGES & BALK

–

Joshua Ferris

was working at a place called Hedges & Balk. It started as a communications firm just south of Columbus Circle, on 7th Ave., floors 40–42. It's no longer around. I drew up reports, press releases, that sort of thing. Sometimes a more specialized project presented itself, a white paper or a product launch, something guerrilla-style. To be honest, there was very little we wouldn't engage with at the start, if a request for proposal came in.

Sometimes it was real to me, other times like a mad cocaine rush. Everyone was pitching new business, everyone hurling themselves across town at a moment's notice. We went up to White Plains, out to New Jersey—where do you need us, how can we be of help? It was the time of our lives for most of us, though we had our fair share of bunglers, too. It wasn't all conquer, conquer, conquer, crush crush crush. Nor was it some cabana in Madagascar. It was business-casual corporate America. It sucked lint balls one-third of the time. Still, we usually had our Sundays. We had our ten days in August down the shore.

This is not really the story of all that. That's the background, the telephone trilling inside some distant office. The real story, my story, took place almost entirely within, amid private moods, subtle shifts in weather. They did their best to bring me along. It didn't always take. I was not always a team player. This is that story.

2.

America was our client. It's grand but true. Caterpillar and Boeing, Anheuser-Busch. We knew the histories, wore the hats. We all had these canted models of the Dreamliner on our desks, sent to us just before its maiden voyage. You go up in the Dreamliner like the princess of Monaco and come down again like John Glenn. It was the myths we were marketing, the canyon curve and prairie dew, the cowboy at dawn with his horse. And then all those we could invent ourselves: Schick versus the Bic Flex 5. The revolutionary Flush 4-in-1 Reviver.

It was kinda fun. We could turn to our loved ones after the slick commercials aired and indulge in a little behind-the-scenes gossip. We were privy to trade secrets, treated like family. Test product arrived and we tore into it. We had blenders going in the kitchens, fake strudel baking in the ovens. We plugged a dryer into the wall socket and stood around listening to its soothing silent hum. Tropicana, Pepsi Cola, Bausch + Lomb.

I love this country. I know that's unfashionable. I mean when left unqualified, without weeding out the worser half. You either give the lie to "united we stand" or stand accused of contributing to its ruin. I refuse to do that, even now. I still hold the whole thing in high regard. I love this country for the sheer spectacle of its daily industry, the dream keeping on down the I-80 corridor. Not to love America is not to love the world.

3.

You'll want to know who I am, the happy one, the one who brought Hedges & Balk down. I can't say I blame you.

But it won't get at anything. Okay, so my name is Robert Blakewood. I stand so many feet tall. How does that get at anything? You're looking for insight into the revolution. What good am I? Okay, so there he is, Robert Blakewood, as slick and unified a human being as Hedges & Balk itself, that inestimable firm. What bullshit. You ask: how old was he? What were his core beliefs? Delve deeply enough, you might strike soul. Pay dirt, baby. Bedrock. Don't blame you. But here's the thing.

Open up a pack of playing cards. Give them a hearty shuffle. One more time for good measure. Now scoot your chair in, square up to the table. Start turning that pack of cards over one at a time. First up is the five of clubs. Next it's the jack of diamonds. Third card is the nine of hearts. Any discernible pattern? Not really. Next couple don't do much to establish one, either. Just one random card after another, it's anyone's guess. Oh, sure, sooner or later, certain patterns do take shape. Any idea why? Neither do I. The seemingly sensible patterns are as random as the acknowledged randomness of the individual cards themselves.

Shuffle, repeat. Go faster, faster. That, it turns out, is the essence of me: I am a random series of moods, each one as vivid as it is inexplicable, and these moods of mine turn themselves over as quickly as the next card can show itself.

To understand how I came to be capable of murder, you don't need my demographics, my shoe size, all that macro data. You need a time stamp on an infinite series. The electro-chemical impulse, synthesis and release, the signal that rides like lightning down the ion channel.

4.

"There are more things in heaven and earth, Horatio, than are dreamt of in your philosophy."

I think of these words from Shakespeare whenever I think of the education I received at H&B. ("From the gully of Hadar to the Xerox machine," Jim Sandydawn used to say, sweeping his fat hand over the office—my Falstaff, my mentor.) It was easy to confuse American enterprise for the Pillsbury Doughboy and the Goodyear Blimp, but a lot of the country's ingenuity went quietly unnoticed. I mean the providers of integrated flow-control solutions and makers of architecture glass, the ten-person organic-snack outfit. It's hard to put a logo on an asphalt shingle. But there were more things, Horatio, in Harrisburg and Chillicothe—and with their wide competitive moats and thirty million in forward sales, they were the last things on earth holding this country together.

They were also our earliest clientele. When I first started at H&B, we didn't yet have our hands on a General Mills or a Xerox Corp., those immortals a dozen brands deep, but it was Jurowski's dream to, and Jurowski discovered me. Paul Jurowski brought me along.

I was living in a cold-water flat in Queens, up to my eyeballs in student debt. I must have looked cute to Jurowski the way a German shepherd pup looks cute in a shop window as it bounds through the shredding. I had been reared on Fugazi and Black Flag, the single-shooter games in cineplexes, and everything on offer at Taco Bell. I harbored the fantasy that I would, one day, be approached by fate, handed a cape on top of a high-rise, and plummet, plummet down the parabola before suddenly soaring off into the blue, my awesome powers new and unknown. My parents were both dead, and I was lonely most of the time.

I was bookish. I liked my news to come in the form of old-fashioned narratives. As a kid, I read every fantasy written about the shipwreck and the stowaway. Before high school was out, I graduated from Stan Lee and the Hernandez Brothers to Baudelaire and Pound, the novels of Joyce and Flann O'Brien. I used to think reading literature was a taste or preference, like choosing Häagen-Dazs over Breyers, a no-brainer, but now I know in America it's never more than a temporary phase and an advertisement for oneself. The first time I walked into H&B, I was half-hungover and carrying the *Collected Stories* of William Faulkner, looking to do nothing more than answer the phone for my sixty percent of $12.50 an hour.

"A little light reading?"

Those were Paul Jurowski's first words to me. Of course I didn't know he was Jurowski at the time. I knew only that he was the man with the shaking and skeletal beast by his side.

"Can anybody here bring a dog into work?" I asked.

"When it's dying of cancer," he said, and sauntered away. The ailing bird dog followed after. I never saw it again.

Even now I don't know why he spoke to me. I was the front-desk temp, tattooed with words, at odds with the target audience. I made no capitulation to the corporate world—the name tags and retreats, the ethical murk of multinationals. Life was too short, and besides, I was better than all that. I suppose, then, this is the story of how I came to think deeply about customer reward points and to drive a BMW.

You grow up. You settle down. You put away childish things.

But at that time I was still living for all-night parties in pop-up locations across Brooklyn and Queens. The flagrant illegality of those wobbly structures was more likely to get you killed than the impromptu mosh pits or pharmaceutical interactions found therein. I partied in water towers, grain silos, abandoned garages. I tranced through houses on duckboards, crowdsurfed with strangers in old churches, went head first into steel beams while the young men on stage whiplashed their hair and bled into microphones. I was never alone in those years, though now I can't remember anyone's name but Cubbie Dexter's. Even their faces are lost to nostalgia and the blur of the crowd.

Cubbie and I would begin the evening with a breakfast of burritos and cheap beer. By the time we were headed out to the main event, the subway car had drained of the doctors and executives and taken on an air of carnival. We soaked our shirts through in hollowed-out lofts and screamed ourselves mute and somehow came through it all sober, high only on adrenaline and the end-times energy of four in the morning. We seemed to be getting more out of life than your average Dan. We knew intimately the deserted dawn hour when the steel doors opened out from the condemned building onto Brooklyn's gray ramparts, the single-use D'Agostino bags fluttering in the barbed wires. The opioid addicts on the park benches, the early joggers lighting out for the water. Depletion and contentment marked those sun-bright evenings, as did the body's need for breakfast. My friends and I, DJs and artists, drug dealers and photographers, would-bes and hopefuls of every stripe and persuasion, sat in Caribbean diners with our ears ringing, hoarse and witless and eating everything in sight. An hour later we were off to our temp jobs and fashion classes, or to home and bed.

There was a little magic to every day, a little unlikely charm. A fillip in the belly that had me convinced that life was only worth living this way: the friends, the fucking, the drugs, the drag-assing, the suffocating poverty, the chill, the thrill, the five a.m. grime. Wasn't this why I'd quit graduate school and why I'd come to the city? Wasn't this how we hoped to avoid regret? America wasn't just the promise of OEM scanners and SKUs. It was the jam band in the basement and the years lost to youth.

In the hot, dusty evenings down from the tracks, we gathered outside the bright storefront galleries for another opening—the men in orange cords and absurd mustaches, the waifs in six ounces of organdy and tulle. Everyone talking, drinking white wine. Hanging from the walls on the inside were our televised childhoods explored with epoxy and twine. We were obsessed with mixed media, the physical properties of flambéed plastics. We pulled shit from the dumpster at the faintest suggestion of glory. We were curious. Were we any good? Almost never. Even on the margins, there was no defending against received ideas. But it did start happening, as I turned 30, for a select few. Gagosian came calling. Cannes offered one or two of us something more than envy. Our friend Hector filmed a romance on the banks of the Gowanus, and six short months later he was the toast of Park City. He took the helm of his first blockbuster sequel at a time I could still barely afford a subway swipe. There were debut novels, breakout performances. The god of fame and commerce raptured the top two percent of us, transfiguring them into angels of the mainstream we'd never hear from again, while the devil took the bottom third down with depression and drugs.

The good times got tweaked, they got twitchy, and I just got tired. I got strung out and old. I lost the will to battle the constant blood sugar dips, the bed-bug scares, the trips to the pharmacy for the morning-after pill. I moved out of Queens. I moved back to Queens. I waited for hours for discount dental work, paging through fashion spreads of people I once knew. I was sick and tired of filching TP from the local Starbucks, hauling it in my socks back to Astoria and squalor. I hadn't known the caress of a clean towel in ten years. Indulgence for me was a bagel with cream cheese. You had to wonder: What's so wrong with the mowed lawns of suburbia? Who can argue with an ergonomic chair?

That was around the time I started temping at H&B, when I still believed in my heart of hearts that I had no grander ambition than to answer the phone.

5.

I'd also lost Cubbie. Cubbie was never cut out for that kind of lifestyle. The hours took their toll, as did the pills, the constant yank and jerk of coming up and going down. Cubbie got sad, lost focus, withdrew. It was hard for him to remember the night the water main broke and we raved to Detroit techno in an icy cold stream, or how we sat shirtless on pallets of cinderblock watching the rising sun compete with the bonfire.

What *was* he cut out for? What was Cubbie Dexter equipped with in life? His mom was in jail, his father unknown. He had no college degree, no skill set or vocation. He was battered by poverty. He was falling apart with diabetes. His hands shook like an old man's. It was never a surprise to find Cubbie on the kitchen floor, desperately trying to regulate his insulin with a bowl of Froot Loops and tap water. He couldn't afford to eat well. He was on a steady diet of Moon Pies and Mountain Dew. Then he'd drop off to sleep for whole days. He lost his job babysitting, lost his girlfriend Joleen, lost his direction completely. His crying jags carried on and on. I found him prone in corners, on stairwells. I'd come up from a day's loading and there he'd be again, and do you know finally how helpless I was? "Cubbie," I'd say, and not knowing what else do to, I'd just curl up with him. I'd curl up with this grown man, this little boy beaten by the big city and his own bad choices, so that he'd know someone loved him. Someone, and I was the world, wanted him to survive. But he was not made for the world. He leapt free of the footpath on the Brooklyn Bridge and threw himself into traffic.

There were girlfriends. There were jobs. There were abrupt changes in scene. Cubbie in a camo kilt and a dope new pair of shoes was my one constant.

Before he killed himself, Cubbie committed nine songs to a 4-track and then refused to upload them to the Internet. It was a piece of genius, I thought, but it wasn't for public consumption. It was for the four walls in Cubbie's bedroom, and twelve fortunate others. For Cubbie transferred this delicate and strange acoustic opus to a dozen cassette tapes and handed them out selectively, sometimes stupidly, as when he gave one unprompted to a hot dog vendor in Prospect Park. (Self-defeating perversity was part of Cubbie's charm.) He never sold one, never promoted it, never even talked about the damn thing. He'd just take a shine to someone and hand off another unlabeled cassette tape— one more in a limited series ... gone.

I listened to Cubbie's album then and I listen to it now. Had I had his talent, I'd have followed a different path. I'd have banged on doors and never taken no for an answer.

Eventually, I let the album fall by the wayside. A few years went by and I found it again, put it on heavy rotation, couldn't believe what he'd done. I have listened only to *Kind of Blue* half so often, only *Blonde on Blonde*, *XO*, *Rumours*, *Ram*. The next time I rediscovered it, two years later, I had cleaned up my act. I was working at Hedges & Balk. It was impossible to find a player. I transferred the tape to CD—something he'd never have done. He was sorry he played the guitar. He wanted to be a poet. Instead he was my private Leonard Cohen. He was my secret and sacred prayer.

I took over for Jim Sandydawn. I bought an apartment, then a building. I moved all my CDs over to digital files later than everyone else. Cubbie's bootleg was lost among 42,000 other items. But when, during a dinner party, or midday at Hedges & Balk, Cubbie came up on shuffle, invariably people would go quiet and say, "Who is this?" I might have told them, but I never did. It was too important. It was too private. I hoarded Cubbie, I kept him all to myself.

Then we flew to Atlanta to pitch a data-capture firm with a market cap of three billion. We stopped into Starbucks for an afternoon pick-me-up, and going in, the furthest thing from my mind being Cubbie Dexter, I gave the homeless man my spare change. Why not? He'd held the door open for us. I was standing with Widener, we were creeping forward in line, we were debating the wisdom of going public, when in among the mints, the macaroons, and the Tony Bennett duets I came across Cubbie Dexter's *Black Heather*. It was no longer an obscurity on cassette tape but a slickly packaged two-disk set with an essay inside penned by John Jeremiah Sullivan. The essay recounted the album's history from obscure cult recording to wide German phenomenon to the top of the Hot 100. I stood there stunned. There was Cubbie, back from the dead and on sale at the Starbucks, and something inside me passed out of this earth forever.

6.

What has been your biggest achievement in the past six months. What has been the most challenging aspect of your work. Name your personal contributions to the team's total goals. Rate your job satisfaction. Can we help you do your job better, quicker, more enjoyably. Where do you see yourself in five years. Do you consider yourself a team player. What would you say are your greatest strengths. Your greatest weaknesses. How often have you arrived late to work. Do you take office supplies home with you. Do you feel you are well-liked. Do you have a specific goal you hope to achieve. How do you see yourself advancing. Do you consider yourself management material. Is there anything you feel we should be concerned about. Is there anything else you would like to add.

7.

"Ask me about William Faulkner."

This was a week or so after our first confab, and I was surprised to find myself still there. He came out of the blue to loom over me suddenly, over the whole front desk, just matter-of-factly right up in my face. I didn't care for it. His clean-shaven cheeks, his perfect head of hair. To live was to be challenged, he seemed to suggest, and his position at the firm, together with the appurtenances, of my interests gave him the liberty to act as my inquisitor. Don't care to be interrogated about Faulkner? Don't bring his *Collected Stories* into a corporate office.

"Is that an employee?" I asked.

"Tell me what you want to know," he said. "Ask me anything."

I didn't care to know anything beyond the words he'd set down on the page 70 years prior: pessimistic accounts of our bedrock nature, the human constraint on progress and learning, the terrible legacies of drunkenness, violence, racial disharmony. So grim a message was, I was guessing, anathema to a brand manager.

"You don't think I know his full name, which was William Cuthburt Faulkner, or when he was born— September 25, 1897—or where—New Albany, Mississippi ... although for most of his life he lived in Oxford, at the estate known as Rowan Oak, a Greek Revival built in the 1840s by architect Robert Sheegog. But everyone knows that. Come on, try harder. Stymie the corporate tool."

"Where's your dog today?" I asked.

"Dead," he said, "like all of the dogs in Faulkner's day."

"Dead? Really?"

"He wrote a total of nineteen novels, 125 short stories, and six collections of poetry, to mention nothing of his essays and screenplays. The eternal return of the past and the crimes of the father visited upon the son are some of his more enduring themes."

"That's very thorough," I said.

He looked off, gesturing as if it were nothing. I became aware, while staring at him, of ghost copies issuing from a nearby machine.

"The point is," he said, "we're not all illiterates here."

"Did I ever say you were?"

"You don't like me, do you?"

"I don't know you," I said. "But it seems you don't like me."

"What's with the tattoos?" he asked. He nodded down at them: EXILE in Roman font along the left forearm, ABIDE along the other. "What's the story there?"

"Maybe when I know you better," I said.

He smiled, knocked twice on the wood and walked away.

"Hey," I said. "I'm sorry about your dog."

"Dogs come and go," he said. It wasn't stoical, exactly. It was just strange, the matter-of-fact reply of a man on the spectrum. He didn't even look back. That was Jurowski. Despite all the years we spent together, I never got used to him, never grew comfortable in his presence. He was supremely odd. Much later, when I leveled the gun at his head, he didn't even flinch.

Chapter 2

OFFICE ENVY

–

Gary Shteyngart

I f you were from a distant galaxy and read contemporary fiction, you might be forgiven for thinking that human beings don't have jobs. There might be some mention of an "office" between the meat of the action, the adulteries and the divorces, the meditations on mortality and the vicissitudes of parenthood, but few contemporary literary novels tackle the 40-plus hours most of us devote to keeping our cupboards stuffed and the kids clothed.

Me, I love work. My first novel began in an office, and my latest book is equally engrossed with office ritual. As a writer, I spend most of my day in bed, typing on a laptop perched atop my stomach, but what I wouldn't give for a little human interaction, a touch of office gossip, a secret meeting by the coffee machine, a well-earned paper cut to remind me I am still alive.

The funny thing is that, when I did have real jobs, I was terribly incompetent at all of them. My first-ever attempt to join the American workforce took place in high school. I was supposed to sell piano lessons on commission in Manhattan's Union Square Park. What this meant was that I would stand in the middle of the park wearing a giant sandwich board shaped like a piano while handing out leaflets advertising piano lessons. I was maybe fifteen, new to Manhattan from the farthest reaches of Queens, and perhaps did not fully understand the nature of the busy commerce of Union Square Park circa 1987.

"Smoke, smoke, trip, trip."

"Horse! I got horse!"

"Get your blow here. Uncut blow. Yessir, I got blow."

"Would you like maybe a piano lesson?"

Needless to say, my commission for the day was zero dollars, although the fact that I am very short probably didn't help, as I was all but swallowed whole by the piano-shaped sandwich board. The other salespeople of the park did a brisk business, and I wish them well in their current pursuits.

A string of other jobs came my way. For a while, I was a janitor at the national nuclear laboratory where my father worked, wearing a badge-like device that was supposed to record the level of radioactivity I received. It was a well-paid job, but I had no idea how to mop or buff a floor and neither did some of the miscreants I worked with. Our major goal was to avoid getting caught by the supervisor who roamed the vast grounds of the national lab in a pick-up truck, complaining about how un-mopped and un-buffed our floors were. We would find a hiding space behind some kind of pulsing science thingy and keep watch for that Ford F-150, meanwhile talking happily of our dreams. I had just seen the movie *Wall Street* and wanted to become a crook; another guy was going to be a bigger star than Michael Jackson. I hated it at the time, but in hindsight this is one of the few jobs from which I didn't get fired or laid off. And I felt close to my goof-off pals. We shared common goals of not wanting to do much, while also fully believing that we were better than the tasks assigned to us. To me that is almost the definition of "work."

I went to a Marxist college that did not offer up many of its graduates to the corporate work force (I won't mention

Oberlin by name), so once I graduated I got a series of nonprofit jobs. I worked for a downtown agency called the New York Association for New Americans, where I wrote brochures for newly arrived Russian immigrants about the importance of good hygiene. In the meantime, I was also writing my first novel, about a hapless worker at a nonprofit agency called the Emma Lazarus Immigrant Absorption Society. (Write what you know, as my high school writing teacher had said.) A small portion of the day was spent attending to my duties—possibly three to four hours a week—while the rest of the time was spent canoodling with my co-workers at an Irish bar, or falling asleep at my desk, or polishing the edges of my novel in progress with great care, somehow combining my creative pursuits within the carapace of a paying job.

I fell in love. Not with a coworker, but with office equipment. I was born in a premodern society, the Soviet Union, so I was easily amazed by the razzle-dazzle of American technology. The Internet was just getting started, but already the office phones were huge and complex and came with an endless array of blinking lights and scrolling LCD screens. How I loved those sleek, gray machines. I would drunkenly run into my office after lunch (it had a stunning view of the Statue of Liberty), jump onto my rolling chair, pluck the receiver off its base, and spin around while the telephone cord wrapped gently and protectively around my body, the dial tone ringing in my ear. The copier was an object of endless fascination. I admit I did not understand how it worked beyond the basic niceties. But the fact that you could put a page with text or graphics on both sides of it, press a button, and out would come a version of both sides of the page dutifully copied and as warm to the touch as a fresh loaf of bread made a great impression on me. I still have no idea how such a thing is possible, but whenever it happens I goggle at the results with an open mouth, like a peasant on his first trip down the mountain into the great, big, steaming city below.

And of course there was the gossip. You picked your friends, just as you did in school, and then for eight hours a day you would talk to them—candidly, breathlessly—about everyone outside your circle. Who was getting promoted, who was about to be fired, who was in love with someone from the far-away-seeming executive floor. Is there any wonder the television show *Mad Men*, about half of which took place within an office environment, was such a hit? Nothing can be more exciting than waltzing into someone's office, dramatically closing the door behind you, as you look your pal in the eye and say, "You are not going to believe this. So-and-so is pregnant/got a bigger office than me/broke the copier." I have lost touch with most of my coworkers, but when I close my eyes I can still feel this incredible energy. Not energy directed at a task, but this great, bubbling, communal energy that comes with being a part of the modern workplace. I can imagine that office workers today are more lost to their screens and their iPhones, but I hope some of that stir-crazy camaraderie still exists, because it is what makes coming to an office so special.

Eventually we were all laid off from that job, and afterward I became a grant writer for another non-profit. There the spirit was more subdued. We wrote grants that got money for all kinds of programs, some of which were actually helpful to various needy constituencies, the elderly and at-risk youth. The Internet, still bulky and charmless, was fully in force at this time, and I spent a lot of my days conducting a doomed love affair with a woman at another non-profit via an exciting new service called Hotmail. All this time, I felt guilty that I wasn't doing enough good work, and since no one got drunk at lunch, it was hard for me to evince any esprit de corps. "Gary's not a team player," was said about me at least once, and it was true. Also, the phones were not as fancy and the copier's product hardly as crisp. Around this time, I sold my first novel, and my days as an office worker were about to come to an end.

So now I work in my bed where, to paraphrase the movie *Aliens*, no one can hear me complain. There are no work parties to attend, no officemates to giggle with, no stale coffee to snag, no office doors to joyfully slam, no breathless secrets to impart. Now I'm just some schmuck in a bathrobe beneath a duvet spinning words into content. Gone is the urgent quack quack quack of the office line. The chirrup-swoosh, chirrup-swoosh of a copier making two hundred copies of a double-sided page in under one hour (yes, I have seen this happen with my own eyes). Soon more and more people will be like me—isolated and strange, grouchy and alone, surrounded by information but without a single soul to share that information with, cheerlessly pressing damp bills into the hands of food deliverers who bring us our daily pad thai, and who will soon themselves be replaced by an army of delivery drones crisscrossing the sky, the last true work colleagues left on earth.

ALONE IN ONE'S ROOM

Sloane Crosley

"There is no gate, no lock, no bolt that you
can set upon the freedom of my mind."

— Virginia Woolf, *A Room of One's Own*

O nce you decide to become an artist (if
you are a certain kind of person, the
decision is made divinely; if you are
another kind, the decision is made by process of
elimination), you're going to need a place to do
it. Writers in particular may not need labs or
dark rooms or human interaction. Our equipment is minimal, our dietary needs limited. But
if you are a writer, eventually you will have to
sit still. Or at least stand still. Thus, despite
our general footloose attitude, space has always
been paramount to us.

"My husband and I had always worked in
the same room," says the narrator of Valeria
Luiselli's story, "Work in the Art of Space."
"More out of lack of money than a surplus of
love." Almost on impulse, they decide to buy
a house in the Bronx (both have their own
concerns regarding the conditions under
which they expect to be productive). Unfortunately, they do so right before leaving the

country to spend the summer traveling with their children. As her story unfolds, Luiselli explores the confounding perplexities of banks and building paperwork, of securing a new home from far away. As in Joshua Ferris's story, the quotidian serves as a foil to the fantastic. Correspondence with mortgage brokers makes for a bracing backdrop to the narrator's ruminations on artistic creation. "The space in which someone works determines, or at least greatly influences, the outcome of what that person produces," says the narrator. Judging by her explorations of Balzac, Picasso, Carravagio, and the very structure of fiction, she's not wrong.

Likewise, Roxane Gay's "The Architecture of Motion" is preoccupied with space, both physical and emotional. She tells the story of Bertrand Grubiani, an architect from New York whose career and personal life are crumbling in a Midwestern city. Still, his work "allowed him a certain freedom the body did not. The structures he designed, he liked to think, moved from his heart to his mind to his hand to the page and into the world." In the midst of upheaval, Bertrand dreams of building not just a room of his own, but an entire house. And as Gay's story builds, so does our curiosity— will Bertrand make his dream house? What changes in us when we attempt to fashion new structures from scratch? Do they lead us to truer and more successful lives or do we simply follow ourselves wherever we go?

"I'm writing this from the Genius Bar of the Mac store," begins Jonathan Safran Foer's "Cargo Plane." The title is a sly nod to this Trojan horse of a story—a story about space within space in the form of an email. The narrator may be typing away in public, but it's really a CD-ROM drive host to all his life's correspondence and creative output that serves as entry point to ruminations on the future, literary allusions, and splashes of autofiction. Unable to sleep after his divorce, the narrator becomes "enamored of lists: facts, untranslatable words from other languages, details." He longs for structure, for assurance that there are more truths to be had than the ones upon which he's built his life. His thirst for information takes a turn for the practical: "I rewired a functioning chandelier. I snaked an unclogged toilet." At one point, he reads a book titled How Architecture Functions. *If these three stories could collide, it's a volume you might find on the shelf of one Bertrand Grubiani.*

"A piece of writing is something that has to be walked into," writes Luiselli. And this is exactly what these stories invite us to do. Here are the ones that seem to whisper, "Step into my office."

Chapter 3

WORK IN THE ART OF SPACE
–
Valeria Luiselli

The children were growing and needed their space; our parents were getting older and had started spending longer periods of time with us. We hadn't really grown, but were of course getting older—just not as fast or as visibly as our parents—and so our needs had also changed.

*

We printed the document and read out loud, taking turns:

> *"Building Description.* This is a wood-frame struc-
> ture that was built in approximately 1890. It is
> a three-story single-family dwelling. The focus
> of our inspection will be to report on the readily
> accessible structural and mechanical components
> of the building and to report any apparent safety
> or health issues." (Old House Inspection Company,
> *Inspection Report*)

*

More than anything, we needed new arrangements in terms of our workplaces, and new agreements in our division of labor-space. My husband and I had always worked in the same room, more out of lack of money than a surplus of love, though we perhaps did learn to love each other more in having to share small spaces—if love can be measured, that is, in the number of things we learn to ignore about the other, and the other to silently tolerate in us. We shared a studio for almost a decade. Having learned to love each other, we agreed, we now each needed to have our own studios. The next step would simply be to find such space—approach it, carefully and slowly, but with certain determination—making sure that it would be an asset in our lives, and not one more liability.

*

> "*Walkways*. The property at the front and side of the building slopes away from the house, which helps to prevent water intrusion. The sidewalk is in fairly good condition. However, one slab has been lifted by tree roots. This situation has caused an alarming trip hazard, which can be a liability. I would recommend that this problem be addressed and the sidewalk be repaired for safety." (Old House Inspection Company, *Inspection Report*)

*

The day my agent called to say I'd be receiving a gener-ous-enough advance for the novel I'd just finished, we opened a bottle of wine, decided to buy a house, and for the first time in years slept more than six hours straight.

Then, that same week, a serendipitous kind of friend phoned us and told us the house next door to his was on sale—a good deal. After a single visit to this house—the only one we saw after we'd made the decision to buy one—and after just one meeting with the owner, it was done.

When we informed our respective parents back in Mexico about our decision to buy a house in New York, my mother said: "Really? And the Trump?"

And my husband's parents said: "Finally! A step forward. Sorry we cannot lend you money."

And my father said: "You are living in an aspirational economy. Think twice."

But we'd already made up our minds. We would buy an old house in the Bronx, even though we hated the idea of leaving Harlem—a neighborhood we had knitted so tightly into our lives as a family that more than a place it seemed like a sort of foundational myth.

*

Then, the Mortgage Bankers wrote:

> "Thank you for choosing us for your home-financing needs. Based on your liquidity events coming up within the next few months we believe you would be best qualified for a lower purchase price, with 75% financing. We would still need to see the receipt of the funds you are receiving for your book advances prior to closing the transaction. Please let us know if you have any questions!"

*

We had many questions, but we put them aside, unleashed the home-buying process, and then cooperated with every

demand that came thereafter. We had made a rash decision, like every important decision we'd taken together up
until then, and now we just had to make up for it. We knew
the drill, at least; we knew how to operate in emergency
mode. In fact, perhaps, we only operate very well when
in emergency mode. And there was a sense of purpose in
this emergency. At the end of all the signing and paying,
and scanning, and sending, and attaching, we'd both have
a house. We'd have a legacy for our children and maybe
our children's children. We'd actually *own* a bathroom and
maybe even a tree—in the Bronx. And more than anything, we'd each be able to work, for as long as we lived,
in our own rooms. Not in the sense of "a room of our own,"
but almost.

*

The only problem was that we'd be leaving New York in
one week's time, to spend three months in a remote place in
Sicily, so any communications we'd have to have—with the
bank, the attorneys, the brokers, the friends and relatives
who might lend us money for the closing costs, the people
we'd have to ask for advice, and the rest of the home-buying
fauna—would have to be at a distance. Had we accurately
foreseen the real complexity of trying to buy an old house
in the Bronx while living in a small town in Sicily—with
no Internet connection, no phones, no printers, no electricity
on some nights—we might not have gone ahead with it.
But then again, should anyone ever be able to foresee how

difficult marriage is going to be, how painful it will be to give birth, how useless a graduate degree can turn out later in life, or how disappointing it might be to cast a ballot, everyone would be living inside a Ziploc bag, next to the broccoli and carrots. We were going to buy that old house, whatever it took, and we'd move into it when we got back to New York in the fall.

*

Then came the Mortgage Bankers, again:

> "There was a discrepancy with one of the bureaus when we pulled Valeria's credit. Is her name Valeria Luiselli or Valeria Luiselli Lopez or Valeria Luiselli Lopez Astrain? Can you please complete the attached form and send back to us so we can get it cleared? Please let us know if you have any questions!"

*

One question I asked myself was, once I had my own studio, would I still write the way I do, or would something change? Something fundamental—in my identity as a writer, as a person, an émigré, a mother, a wife?

Though I've had to learn to live and write in just about any space and situation, I've always attached a kind of aura to writing spaces. I've always held the belief—though I realize this belief belongs to the category of magical think-ing—that the space in which someone works determines, or at least greatly influences, the outcome of what that per-son produces.

For this same reason, as I writer, I've always envied artists' studios. If I were able to choose a specific type of workspace to write in, it would be full of canvases, oil paints, and half-finished sculptures. I think I can trace my fetish for artists' studios to one precise origin, and that is Balzac's story *Le Chef-d'œuvre inconnu*, published in 1831. The story portrays a tense power struggle among three artists at distinct "moments" of their career: the young, promising Nicolas Poussin; the accomplished, mature artist François Porbus; and the aging, forgotten and bitter has-been Maître Frenhofer. The story takes place in 1612, and is partly set in Porbus's studio, on Rue des Grands-Augustins, in Paris. The young Poussin lingers outside the studio for a while before he dares to knock on the artist's door: "He went up and down the street before this house with the irresolution of a gallant who dares not venture into the presence of the mistress whom he loves for the first time...." After Poussin finally gathers enough courage, and walks into the artist's studio, the space is described as a kind of genius mess: "Plaster *écorchés* stood about the room; and here and there, on shelves and tables, lay fragments of classical sculpture-torsos of antique goddesses, worn smooth as though all the years of the centuries that had passed over them. The walls were covered, from floor to ceiling, with countless sketches in charcoal, red chalk, or pen and ink. Amid the litter and confusion of color boxes, overturned stools, flasks of oil, and essences, there was just room to move so as to reach the illuminated circular space where the easel stood."

Every time I read the description of that studio, I am Poussin all over again, pacing up and down the street, waiting to gather enough courage to knock on the door.

*

I will never have a studio like the one Balzac described, just like I will never buy all those beautiful things that stationery stores sell—because how would I justify cobalt blue and an easel-cleaning liquid? But once I had a house, a house with a basement, I thought, I'd have a proper space, a real foundation for the printing workshop I'd always dreamed of having. I'd just need to buy a movable-type printing press, and learn how to write backward. Then I would be able to publish wondrous little books by writers I love, and give them to my friends as they swayed out our door after long, generous dinner parties, before they disappeared into a dark street on a humid summer night.

*

"*Basement.* We could not evaluate the foundation walls. However the basement appeared to be sound, stable, and was dry at the time of inspection. The small glimpses of the foundation we could find showed no bulging or cracking and no evidence of water intrusion was present." (Old House Inspection Company, *Inspection Report.*)

*

Like most people I know, we'd been priced out of our neighborhood, Hamilton Heights, in Harlem, where we'd lived for almost a decade. For this fact, I hold a little grudge against L.M. Miranda and his otherwise wonderful Broadway hit, *Hamilton*. Since the play began cashing in millions, our neighborhood, home to the real Alexander Hamilton, had filled with places named after him—Hamilton Pub, Hamilton Grill, Hamilton Yoga, et cetera—and these places immediately filled with people, who materialized in the span of a single summer, equipped with their laptops, crocks, rolled-up yoga mats, and trust funds.

*

The Mortgage Bankers wrote:

> "In regards to the 4506T form, you did not check the attestation box to the left above the signature lines. I have attached another copy for you to complete. Please print, check, sign, and send back. Please let us know if you have any questions!"

My husband, in reply to the Mortgage Bankers:

> "Yes, we do have more questions. With this kind of mortgage, can we make advances without getting punished?"

Me, in reply-all to my husband and the Mortgage Bankers:

"He means: advance *payments*. Just to clarify."

*

The Balzacs and Mirandas are always to blame. A few centuries before Miranda ruined Hamilton Heights, Balzac had also contributed to a large, future real estate bubble by means of the same procedure: endowing property with added value by means of representing it or its inhabitants inside an artwork—literary, visual, or of any other sort. In the early 1930s, the mime artist and director Jean-Louis Barrault had sought out the same studio in the Rue des Grands-Augustins that appeared in Balzac's story, possibly because of its literary/historical value, and paid a considerable monthly rent to be able to rehearse his plays in it. Then, in 1937—approximately 325 years after Poussin walked into Porbus's house, and 95 years after Balzac published his final version of this story—Picasso decided to rent the same Rue des Grands-Augustins studio. He claimed that the ghost of Balzac had haunted him ever since he read *Le Chef-d'œuvre inconnu*, and was so transfixed by the story that he decided to live and work in the very same space where Balzac set the story. (It was there, in the fictional site of *Unknown Masterpiece*, that Picasso painted *Guernica*.)

Balzac was a pioneering gentrifier of this once-quiet and unremarkable street. Then came Barrault, then Picasso, both falling for the bait. In sum, the main culprits of real estate inflation tend to be writers and artists, but they are also the first victims of their meddling with interest rates. Today, a two-bedroom apartment in the Rue des Grands-Augustin costs €1,500,0000 and a brownstone in Hamilton Heights costs over $4,000,000, and it is unlikely that any real writer or artist will ever live there again.

*

"*Living Spaces*. Each of these spaces has been provided with an adequate number of electric outlets. We tested the outlets that were available. These outlets proved to be wired correctly and were properly grounded. However we observed one outlet in each of the upper bedrooms that was showing an open ground." (Old House Inspection Company, *Inspection Report*.)

*

Once Picasso rented that studio space on Rue des Grands-Augustin, he bought an old hand press that had belonged to Louis Port. "Now that I have a room, I brought it here," he said. All his engravings, after that, were printed in that old hand press. Perhaps with an air of grandiose confidence, which at times waned into simple optimism, and then dimmed further into mere realism, I dreamt of having my own letter press in the very intestines of our future house. I could eventually print all kinds of masterpieces there, every as of yet untranslated poem or story in Spanish, anything I wanted. But what were the intestines of this new home and what was in them?

*

My husband and I leafed through the "Mechanics" section of the old house inspection document, which we had with us all the while, like a kind of Bible or *I Ching*:

> "*Heat.* An oil-fired steam boiler supplies the heat for the building. Steam rises to the cast iron radiators throughout the house for distribution. We tested the boiler which was running at the time of inspection. However the boiler is old and probably inefficient. There is no way to speculate on how long the boiler will service."

> "*Potable Hot Water.* A gas-fired 50-gallon hot-water heater provides the hot water for domestic use. Each fixture was receiving ample hot water quickly at the time of inspection."

> "*Plumbing.* No leaking or unusual moisture was observed anywhere in the building."

*

As my husband and I read through the inspection document, we wondered constantly about how all these deeper things would express their existence in our future house—heat, potable water, electricity, plumbing, gas—but especially, though we never confessed it to each other, about how all these things would feed into our lives in our new, respective and future studios. My husband, I realized as he flipped through the pages of the document, had a different sort of fetish with regard to work spaces, but a fetish nonetheless. And what he expected from the property we were in the process of purchasing was informed by it.

But what was it, exactly, that he imagined and wanted? Though we had been talking about the subject for weeks, I only understood him more clearly one morning, during a two-day stop in Naples on our way to Sicily.

We met old friends there, in Naples, and made plans to see the city together. These friends—a long-married couple who had two children later in life and thus treated them sometimes like tenants, sometimes like aging cats, sometimes like plants, and other times, though fewer, like a chronic illness—had suggested the plan. Why not spend the morning chasing Caravaggio around the city? And we had keenly agreed to this, not so much because we thought it was a perfect plan, not because we loved these particular friends very much and appreciated their company and conversation more than we do most other persons', but because we see our kids in a similar way, and thus under-stand and respect all parents that treat their offspring like the perplexing strangers that they in fact are.

We knew that it would be a rigorous, if not difficult, but also perfect day, cajoling both theirs and ours—a ladder of four children, ranging in age from five to eleven and in personalities from manageable to highly aggravating—around the city's churches, looking up at paintings. So before we set off, we gave the four little tenants a decent-enough breakfast—coffee, bread—and gave our-selves more than one espresso. Once on our way, my husband instantly assumed a role that, we all discovered, suited him well: something between museum guide, kin-dergarten teacher, and Gestapo officer. As we walked into the small, circular chapel on the Via dei Tribunali to see the first Caravaggio, he rounded the children up and sat them on the pews in front of the painting. For what seemed like a beatific and almost long-enough while, he paused their nagging, their seemingly endless and always-urgent desire for something not quite providable, their general, metaphysical itch. The four tenants were now gathered around and somewhat under him, like little apples pulled and pinned down to the ground by a gravitational miracle. They were a sight. They were beautiful and memorable. Had they had better parents, they would have been photo-graphed, photocopied, maybe Instagrammed.

They looked up, agape, at Caravaggio's enormous *The Seven Works of Mercy*, which occupies the altar space in the chapel, and my husband walked them through its many

collage-like layers, as well as the slow process of their coming into being. On the upper left-hand corner, the angel
of mercy, ensuring that merciful deeds are being properly performed on earth. Every now and again, he would
interrupt his own train of thought to say, "The light!"
And there, he pointed, with his back to us, sitting on
the ground, was the sick man whose pain would soon be
alleviated by the pious passerby; the skin on his back,
yellow-green around the cervical bones, and waxing ash-
gray as the back descends toward the lumbar bones. The
children had then insisted on hearing more about the old
man in the painting who, peering from a jail cell at the
bottom right-hand corner, was sucking on the breast of a
young woman, drops of milk clinging to his graying beard
like a stone about to finally break off from a steep cliff. But
my partner had decided against explaining material that
was overtly erotic, pornographic, or even political, so he
simply shrugged and said: "That's not the point."

"So what's the point then?" asked our eldest, who was
almost twelve, but still eleven.

"The point is the light."

"What do you mean, Pa?" the eldest insisted.

But my husband did not explain himself then,
because the youngest of the four had just realized she had
gotten a splinter from rubbing her little palm against the
pew, and then erupted into a wild form of weeping that
involved loud wails, sighs full of seemingly real melancholy, and a series of robust tears. So we all gathered up
again, made for the exit, and stepped out into the blazing
mid-summer's light in search of a pair of tweezers.

*

"*Deck.* A luminous deck can be accessed from the first floor. We observed a sway and apparent sagging in the deck structure as well as signs of wear. I would recommend having the deck repaired or replaced by a qualified contractor for safety. He may be able to brace or re-enforce from below." (Old House Inspection Company, *Inspection Report.*)

*

Again, the Mortgage Bankers:

"There was an unusual system error in regards to the previous 4506T form we had you complete. As a result we will need you to fill out another copy for us. Please let us know if you have any questions!"

As we made our way through narrow streets, looking for a pharmacy where we might find tweezers, the little tenants had many questions. That's basically what tenants have. The questions ranged from very smart to less so:

How did Caravaggio mix his paints?

Who made the costumes for the models?

Can we get another ice cream after this?

The point is the light, my husband repeated later that morning, when we had finally found the tweezers, relieved the little one from her splinter, and stopped in a café—

another coffee for us four, and a scoop of ice cream for the children. The way he explained it to the children was something like this: Caravaggio used to paint inside a mostly dark room, in which the single source of light was a hole he'd made on the ceiling. This concentrated beam of light illuminated his models directly and dramatically from above, at an angle. Then, he'd place a camera oscura in front of them, through which the light passed, refracted, inverted the image, and projected it onto his canvas. To start, he'd make a few markings on the canvas using the sharpened tip of his blade—here the nape of this Madonna; here the elbow of her son, Jesus; here the heel of the beggar. Then, without further markings or traces—no charcoal, no pencil—he'd start using the colors previously mixed and prepared on the palate, painting on top of the images of his models projected on the canvas through the camera oscura. Caravaggio, basically, made photocopies of his models, in order to re-represent images well inscribed in Catholic mythology and legend.

The little tenants now had more questions about the light: But how did the camera oscura project the light? Why didn't he just take a picture?

We paid and then continued walking, slowed down by the increasing density of people, motorbikes, stalls, and café tables. Perhaps what Caravaggio was doing, quite literally, was painting with light. Or maybe simply painting light but not in the slightly tacky way of the Impressionists. He was trapping light—between the canvas and successive layers of oil paint.

*

"*Walls & Ceilings.* The walls and ceilings are painted plaster and possibly drywall where repairs or renovation may have been done. As with any older home you will need to do the usual repair of holes where pictures and such are removed when the house is vacated as well as rough spots around outlets and light switches." (Old House Inspection Company, *Inspection Report*)

*

In the early 1930s, Brassaï, the Hungarian photographer whom Henry Miller later nicknamed "the Eye of Paris," photographed some of Picasso's sculptures for André Breton's Surrealist art magazine, *Minotaur*. And so, for a period, Brassaï visited the painter on a regular basis. He took hundreds of pictures of the work, but his best photographs are of Picasso's sculptures, using only the light emanating from an oil lamp. After each visit to Picasso's studio, Brassaï would return home, make copious notes on his talks with Picasso on little scraps of paper, and stuff them into a giant vase. Like an Ariadne chasing a lone, over-testosteroned Minotaur in his self-made labyrinth, Brassaï observed and documented every little thing about Picasso's work spaces and the way he inhabited them, both through his lens and in those notes. For example, according to Brassaï, Picasso was in the habit of not throwing away the empty boxes of cigarettes, which he so fervently smoked. They were placed, one upon the other, forming tall cardboard towers, which surrounded his early sculptures and collections of objects, and which perhaps made his studio resemble a kind of palimpsestic collage of an old Roman city that had quickly waxed Byzantine, was later conquered by Normans, and was finally dreamt of in Salvador Dali's luminous and paranoid little head. Or, for example, according to Brassaï, Picasso refused to clean or let anyone clean his studio, because he was convinced that dust was the only material on earth that seriously and successfully preserved art—"Just you remember Pompeii," he would argue.

*

"*Bathrooms.* No leaking or evidence of moisture was observed under the sinks or toilets. However a few issues will need to be addressed." (Old House Inspection Company, *Inspection Report*)

*

As the summer matured and the days advanced, so did the stages of our home-buying process, though it seemed like nothing really moved or changed at all. There were always more little things to be done, a myriad, which amounted to a sense of impossibility. In small cafés and bars, we asked impatient waiters for Wi-Fi passwords and then typed hurried, worried replies, again and again; we held on to our USB drive as if it were a buoy in the middle of the ocean; we developed a sixth sense for tobacco or stationery stores with access to Xerox printers; and we even learned to download apps with which to scan documents with our phones. We learned, in other, more comforting words, to capture light in ways Caravaggio might have envied.

*

And then, once more, the Mortgage Bankers:

> "If you are borrowing money from someone else to facilitate the purchase of real estate, as many people do, we would need to understand if there are repayment obligations, which could adversely impact your ability to qualify. Please let us know if you have any questions!"

And my husband to the Mortgage Bankers:

> "That's why I asked for clarity in my previous mail, dear Dick. Please consider that I'm not an accountant in further communications. But I'm taking care of it."

And the Mortgage Bankers:

> "We are missing the second page of your Schedule

C from your 2016 Tax Return. 'Schedule C' will be noted in the top left corner. If your niece in New York is unable to locate these pages, maybe it would be easier if she scanned the entire document. Please let us know if you have any questions!"

And my husband to the Mortgage Bankers:

"Yes, we do have one more question. What is Schedule C?"

*

But we had many more questions than that, of course. For instance, what is a house, really? And what do you do with one once it's yours? And how will living in a house, our own house, change the way we live? Will we be more stable? And also, dear inspector, dear mortgage bankers, will we write good novels in that house? And how? Can you give us any guarantee, any instructions to follow beyond this transaction?

A novel needs a roof, floors, doors, and stairs. A roof is a voice, either providing comfort or imposing a sense of oppression. Floors are pure syntax, sometimes thin and even, others full of gaps. Doors provide rhythm beyond syntax, the possibility to execute changes in time and mood. Stairs connect and divide. But a good novel, more than anything, needs good windows.

Will we get all this when we purchase the house? The mortgage bankers would have no answers, this at least we knew.

*

So we consulted the Old House Inspection Company *Inspection Report,* and this is what it said:

"*Roof.* We were not able to access the roof."

"*Floors.* The floors are covered; therefore we could not get a look at the structure of the floor system. However as we moved through the house we found no reason to question the floor's stability. No unusual movement was observed. The majority of the flooring throughout the building is wood. Some vinyl was observed and may be out dated. The wood floors are in good condition but are showing some wear. No loose or cupped boards were observed, and no unusually wide gaps were noted. Wood floors can always be refinished."

"*Doors.* As with any older home that has not been renovated or restored the doors are lacking maintenance. Many doors rub at the top, side, or bottom."

"*Stairs.* The stairs throughout the building are constructed of wood and appeared to be sound and stable. These stairs have been equipped with the required continuous handrails, which were found to be properly secured."

*

But a good novel, more than anything, needs good windows. Toward the end of the summer, our friend K. M. Alcott visited us for a few days, and we took her to one of our preferred beaches, in the northwestern coast of the Tyrrhenian— dramatic, capricious, and beautiful. She and I were sitting on some high, jagged rocks, while my husband and the two kids snorkeled below. There, she read a short story out loud to me. The two of us were in the process of editing our respective manuscripts, so were particularly sensitized to any display of seriously good syntax. The story, by Antonio Di Benedetto, is called "Abandonment and Passivity," and begins with a burst of light specking a drawer in a room. We spent that afternoon, and then that night, and then the next morning, intermittently but with absolute commitment, discussing the details of this story. I suspect we each liked it for different reasons—who knows if professional, or personal, or both—but it gathered us around its own particular light the way people gather around a fireplace, to be both silent and in company.

The story is about a woman who leaves a man. But there is no woman in the story, and no man. What there is, is a room. A room where there's a suitcase full of personal items that then leaves the room. After that, in that room, there's only a glass of water, and a note pressed under it, against the flat surface of a wooden bedside table. There's also a vase with feverishly red flowers, and a windup clock that soon stops ticking, and also a wooden chair. And finally, there's a fly that flies from sun to sun, from sun to sun—"but only twice," the narrator specifies.

We spent a while, perhaps longer than was deserved, discussing the problem posed by that "but only twice." Alcott has one of those minds that will not abandon an idea until it has squeezed every last bit of sense out of it, or until it is distracted by something larger and more holy.

Theory number one: the sun only illuminates the fly twice because a fly only lives 48 hours, so the narrator is indicating that time is passing (accelerating the story's chronology with a single, brilliant stroke). But neither of us were sure if a fly indeed lives for that amount of time. Theory number two: outside the room, the day is cloudy but the sun behind the mass of clouds is strong and penetrating, so that when a gap of blue opens in between the passing clouds, the sun's direct light illuminates the fly's trajectory, making it twice visible for the spectator in an unspecified, but possibly small amount of time—sun to sun, sun to sun. In any case, from all this, the only certain conclusion that we were able to deduce and agree upon was that, most importantly, in that suddenly abandoned room, there is a window, a wide, generous, and solid window through which light passes, illuminating this vivid *nature morte* as time passes through it—I think that I said "through" it and she said perhaps "across" it, but it might have been the other way around. And this light-in-time, slowly but relentlessly, does the only thing that it knows how to do, which is to render all the objects obsolete, and to reveal a kind of intrinsic sadness in all of them.

Where is the narrator standing in this story? That's the question that really obsessed us, I think. But we never said so out loud. We were wearing two-piece swimming suits, and sweating copiously, and so perhaps felt under-entitled to be posing such questions. But we felt lost in the story, in a way that one writer, reading another, cannot bear to feel. The problem, I argued, though I do not know if Alcott ever agreed with me, is that the narrator in this story, and therefore the reader, *is* the window. I tried to make my case, as my partner and the children were making their way back up toward us. Then, when I finished speaking, Alcott smiled, excused herself, and jumped into the illuminated sea from a high and very dangerous rock.

*

One day, looking through the photographs of Paris he had taken in the early 1930s—pimps, prostitutes, dive bars, opium dens, brothels—Picasso told Brassaï: "When one sees what you express through photography, one realizes everything that can no longer be the concern of painting. Why would the artist stubbornly persist in rendering what the lens can capture so well?"

Until this point, Picasso's comments seem not only reasonable enough but even outdated. What is striking is what he says next: "Photography came along at a particular moment to liberate painting from literature of all sorts, from the anecdote, and even from the subject."

I've always wondered about this—rather irritating—

commentary, and why Picasso's view of literature was that of a kind of secondary art form, limited to anecdotal representation and enslaved by subject matters.

*

"*Windows.* I would recommend cleaning and lubricating window tracks to improve gliding and locking operations. You may need help from a window-repair company." (Old House Inspection Company, *Inspection Report*)

*

Perhaps Picasso was right about the particularities and the differences between painting, photography, and literature, but maybe not for the right reasons. It may be that literature is a form that, despite its roofs, its floors, doors, stairs, and all the other necessary, worldly paraphernalia, indeed lacks windows. Or, to be more accurate, it lacks window-ness. One cannot look through or even into a novel or a piece of writing the way one stands before a painting or a sculpture—and be hit by it, in one single, direct blow. A piece of writing is something that has to be walked into, gone through and across, and sometimes even thoroughly inspected, appraised, and inhabited before it can render any meaning. That is exactly why writing and reading are so difficult, slow, strenuous—and also better than anything else.

But that is also why a writer might ask—and what

if this novel had windows? What if a novel could both be experienced the way a painting is, in one single take, and then, also like a painting, more slowly, examined and inspected?

*

Possible future email from us to a window-repair company:

Dear Window-Repair Specialist,
Caravaggio painted all his best canvases in a dark room, illuminated only by a single source of light—in the roof. Later, Brassaï took the best pictures of Picasso's sculptures, with only the light emanating from an oil lamp. We will not bore you with illustrative examples. The point is, we have been writing novels all our lives, and are now aging. So we have been wondering, Could you come and lubricate our windows? We do not ask anything more than just this. We do not want anything permanent or too complex. And we have no money to pay you, either. Just give us a window, and we will give you one last story.

Chapter 4

THE ARCHITECTURE OF MOTION
–
Roxane Gay

ertrand Grubiani, Bert for short, believed buildings moved. While in architecture school at Cooper Union in New York City, he sat on bus benches staring at skyscrapers. If he looked hard enough, he could see them swaying against the horizon, and that suggestion of movement filled him with something like faith. Bertrand, who went by Bert because people seemed to be uncomfortable with his given name, no longer lived in New York, but often, while driving to work, he would look at his small Midwestern city's architectural offerings with a sense of longing and a little, or a lot, of desperation. The buildings were passionless, drab, and unassuming. They were quotidian and reminded him far too much of the three-bedroom, split-level home he shared with his wife, Brenda. They made him question his faith.

Alicia, Bert's mistress—and how he loved the sound of that word, "mistress," and how holding that word on his tongue made him feel like a different, better man—said Brenda reminded her of the lawyer's wife in the movie *Pretty Woman*, a woman whose ass could melt ice. Whenever she told him this, Bert snickered, imagining Brenda lying on her twin bed, ass in the air, an ice cube perched atop, slowly changing states of matter.

Every morning before work, Bert stood in front of his office building, hoping one of the buildings around him might move, even a little. Then he would head to his office, wheezing slightly as he patted his jacket pocket for his inhaler, a device he hated because it reminded him of his respiratory impotence. It was humbling to have such ambition and visions of grandeur, coupled with an inability to reach for things greater than himself. His work, however, allowed him a certain freedom that his body did not. The structures he designed, he liked to think, moved from his heart to his mind to his hand to the page and into the world. It was a small, slightly bitter consolation.

Few people could tell Bert had such passion throbbing beneath his slight frame. Bert studied the sign for his firm, GRUBIANI AND SONS. The name was Brenda's idea, in the hope that forward thinking would increase the mobility of Bert's sperm. Such was not the case. After seventeen years of marriage, they remained childless, instead devoting their attention to their poodle, Cookie. It took time for Bert to develop anything more than antipathy for the dog, but as the years passed, his awe for Cookie's longevity developed into an uncomfortable affection. Nodding to a coworker, Bert entered the building, mentally preparing for his day, the only bright spot a potential quickie with Alicia pressed up against the dusty blinds of his office.

The last part of his day's itinerary was wishful thinking at best. Alicia was increasingly apathetic to Bert's affections—a fact that gnawed around the edges of Bert's heart. But he ignored the sensation, telling himself it was heartburn, telling himself her current state of apathy was no different than the apathy she had demonstrated toward him for the past few years. Alicia regarded him the same way he regarded Cookie—with uncomfortable, distant affection.

As he sat behind his desk, he removed his jacket and rolled up his sleeves, swiveling around to stare at the blueprints on the drafting table adjacent to his desk. It was his dream home—a project he had been working on for years. He became so absorbed in his reverie he didn't hear the knock on his door. When a throat cleared, he looked up, rubbing his eyes.

"I didn't hear you come in," he said, smiling nervously, hoping maybe he would get that quickie after all.

Alicia shrugged. "I knocked."

Bert tried to cover the blue prints with his right arm. The house was his secret, and he was strangely protective of the design, of the hope seeping from the inked edges of the structure.

"I'm thinking we need to talk."

Bert wheezed loudly, shook his inhaler, and sucked on the mouthpiece so hard he could imagine swallowing it whole. "Us?"

Alicia fingered the pencil jar on the edge of Bert's desk. "We're not going to see each other anymore."

Bert took another stab at his inhaler, regretting the decision to come to work—regretting, in fact, a whole pattern of decisions leading up to this very moment. "We aren't?"

"Our thing isn't working for me anymore."

"I rather enjoy our relationship."

"It's time to move on."

Bert wasn't surprised or offended. Alicia was always dry, emotionally circumspect. He felt another empty space forming inside him, next to the spaces for his unborn children, what his marriage should have been, and where his career had derailed. He feared that soon there would be nothing but a dry, empty cavity beneath his cheap dress shirt. "Can we stay friends?" he asked quietly.

Alicia reached across the desk and took hold of Bert's hand, bringing it to her lips. "We were never friends." Alicia picked up the single picture of Brenda on Bert's desk. "Did she ever find out about us?"

"My wife doesn't know anything about me," Bert said.

"We are the two loneliest people I know."

Bert turned back around and loosened his grip on his inhaler. "I don't know what to say to that."

Alicia came around the desk and kissed Bert softly on his bald spot, then brushed her lips across his. Ignoring the shiver down his spine, Bert smiled, cupping her chin in his hands. "Do you even like me?"

"Yes, I like you."

"Will you be quitting?" Bert asked.

"Are you firing me?"

He shook his head, forcing a tight smile. "You're one of my best architects. Go. Work. Earn your living, have a nice life."

Alone, Bert stared at the dusty blinds, bent and sagging. His chest tightened, and he briefly entertained the possibility that he was about to suffer a heart attack. Eventually, he realized he was not that lucky. His breathing stilled, and he forced himself to ignore the sounds of his office, concentrating on the steady, if not slower, softer beating of his heart. For the second time in his life, Bert started to cry, not just a masculine and stoic reddening of the eyes, but deep sobs he choked into his trembling hand as his face puckered miserably.

Seven years into his marriage to Brenda, and four days after the fertility specialist informed they it was Bert's fault that the couple couldn't conceive, he came home from work to find their queen-sized bed replaced by two twin beds, neatly made up with matching bedspreads. "You snore too much and I need my space," Brenda told him. "And I'm no longer attracted to you." That night, Bert moved into the guestroom, where he could snore and masturbate in peace. As he lay sleeping, alone for the first time since the day they were married, he couldn't get over how small he felt, the largeness of the bed, the coldness of the house. Tears welled in the corners of his eyes, and an ache in his chest lodged itself there permanently. That was the first time Bert cried.

The rest of Bert's day passed quickly, but no matter how many eye drops he used, his eyes stayed red. An allergic reaction to dust, he told his staff. When five o'clock came, Bert stood in the doorway of his office, watching the staff hover around the elevators, fortifying himself for an evening at home, now that his other option was no longer an option, even though he still very much wanted it to be.

*

"What's for dinner?" Bert asked, as he sat at the kitchen table in a worn T-shirt and Bermuda shorts.

Brenda slowly stirred something in a large pan. "We're having gazpacho."

"Isn't that supposed to be served cold?"

"You're a cook, now? I'm trying something new. I'm improvising, like those handsome boys on the Food Network."

Bert grimaced, protectively covering his stomach with one hand.

Brenda turned down the heat and pulled a roasted chicken out of the oven. As Bert sliced the meat, he looked Brenda up and down. She scowled, removed her apron, set the hot gazpacho abomination on the table, and sat across from him, looking both bored and annoyed. It was remarkable, he thought, the range of moods she was able to express between her eyebrows and her lips. After spearing some meat onto his plate, he sat down, pushing food around his plate. Smiling, Brenda poured a large ladle of the soup over Bert's chicken, then served herself. Bert glared across the table, clenching his knees together. His nose wrinkled at the unidentifiable odor and the odd colors congealing over the once-appealing chicken. He thought of Alicia's lips, cool and tight, pressed against his in the office, and the prospect of spending another night in the guestroom. It was, perhaps, a fine time for a heart attack, after all. Bert pushed his plate away.

"I'm not hungry."

"That's your problem, Bert."

"I've had about enough of being told what my problems are for one day."

"You haven't heard it enough if you keep doing the same things over and over, day after day, year after year. After year."

Bert jammed his fork into the entire piece of chicken and brought into his mouth, gnawing off a large chunk. "Are you happy?" he asked, his mouth full of food.

Brenda smiled triumphantly.

Bert spit the food back onto his plate. "You never could cook."

Brenda took a dainty bite of her food, then dabbed her lips with the corner of a napkin. "You never could give me children."

Bert sat silently watching his wife finish her dinner. She was a beautiful woman, but she did herself no favors while she ate, lips greasy, eyes vacant, teeth bared. As she swallowed the last bite, he carefully folded his napkin and set it atop his plate. Cookie yapped in the next room. He fixated on a clump of mascara dangling from one of Brenda's eyelashes.

"I want a divorce."

"Is this another one of your mid-life crises? 'Let's buy some land and build our dream house. Let's adopt a kid. Let's move back to New York.' Now it's a divorce?"

"I'm leaving tonight."

It was strange, Bert thought, that he had just now discovered his spine, and a fairly formidable spine it was.

"What about Cookie? You're not taking my baby!" Brenda said in a shrill voice.

"I hate the dog."

Brenda's eyes narrowed. "It's going to cost you to leave me."

Bert's eyes felt unnaturally dry. "It would cost me to

stay." His entire body was sore, but all he could do was laugh as Brenda's face grew first red and then a dark shade of purple, the clump of mascara falling onto the tip of her nose. Grunting, he pulled the thin gold band from his finger and dropped it in the gazpacho. It was the first time Bert ever removed his wedding ring. The skin beneath the ring looked clammy and gray.

*

Bert packed his things and moved to the Embassy Suites, a prefabricated hotel that did little to complement the downtown skyline. When he checked in, Bert stood in front of the hotel, squinting as he stared upwards, hoping the building might move, if even just an inch, to welcome him to his new life. The structure stared back at him, refusing to budge. Bert's shoulders sagged.

His room was nice enough, if not a bit too large, and he spent the first few minutes exploring his new home and executing the customary confiscation of the pen and stationery, complimentary toiletries and coffee packets. And then, alone in a strange, antiseptic place, the weight of his day, all its losses, settled on Bert's shoulders and in his chest. He lay on the bed, too tired even to remove his shoes. It took no time at all for him to fall into a dreamless sleep.

In the morning, Bert lazily flipped through the phone book looking for an attorney. True to her word, Brenda had already hired one of her own, and she had left several threatening messages with his secretary. It was only ten a.m., but he understood his soon-to-be ex-wife's anger —neither of them would have imagined him to be the one to find the initiative to disrupt the stale ennui of their marriage.

Choosing a firm at random, Bert called and made an appointment for that afternoon. Nervously, he paced his hotel room until three o'clock, when he walked the three blocks to the law offices of Vreeland, Agnacci, and Stoltz. The building was hideous—low to the ground, too many windows, no personality. He didn't even bother hoping the building might quiver. Buildings where marriages ended were unlikely to understand motion.

The lawyer, Ursula, was pregnant—so pregnant she had to wedge herself behind her desk and take a deep breath before speaking. Bert took a hit from his inhaler, smoothed his hair, tried to still his trembling hands. "I need to get a divorce."

Ursula threw her hands in the air. "Slow down."

"You're very pregnant."

Ursula arched an eyebrow. "You noticed. Do you have any children?"

Bert tried to squelch a pang of envy as a spray of acid burned at the back of his throat. "No, though increasingly I consider that a blessing."

Ursula made a note on the legal pad in front of her. "What's your story?"

"I've been married for seventeen years, and now I don't wish to be married any longer."

"Adultery?"

Bert paused, remembering the hollow nausea he felt every time he saw the twin beds in his wife's bedroom. "Mutual indifference."

Ursula smiled.

"I feel like I'm talking to a therapist."

"I am your lawyer, therapist, friend, and whatever else it takes to make this divorce as painless as possible for you."

Bert scratched his forehead. "My wife, she hates me. In her words, I'm a pathetic little man. We don't have kids because I can't give her any, and she holds it against me. We have a dog on death's door, and we haven't slept in the same room, let alone the same bed, for the past twelve years."

"Have you been faithful to your wife?"

Bert looked away. "No."

"Does your wife know?"

"No."

"How many indiscretions?"

Bert closed his eyes. He could see Alicia, the lean slope of her back, the soft patch of hair on the back of her neck, her lips on his hand kissing him goodbye. "I had one affair, for three and a half years. She left me the same day I told my wife I was divorcing her," he said, his voice cracking.

"So the divorce is your idea?"

"Yes."

For the next hour, Ursula asked Bert the kind of questions he once would have never dreamed of needing to answer. When he finished talking, he said, "I only want one thing—the land we bought."

Ursula made some more notes, groaning softly. "This is a good start. I'd like to say things will go smoothly, but divorce is divorce. It rarely goes smoothly." Setting her pen down, she blew her bangs out of her face. She looked so young, Bert thought, too young to deal with ugly, broken marriages for a living.

Bert's shoulders felt heavier than ever. He was losing the foolish rush of confidence he felt when he tossed his wedding ring into his wife's absurd gazpacho. As he left the lawyer's office, he could hear his heart careening from side to side in the empty cavity of his chest. There was nothing holding him in place.

Bert and Brenda married in Queens, New York, where they shared a small studio apartment while Bert worked his way through architecture school. They found a small Catholic church, breathtakingly Gothic, on Astoria Boulevard, and spent six weeks in marriage counseling with Father Daniel O'Shaughnessy. Bert never forgot that detail, mostly because the priest always reeked of cheap wine and had a tendency to stare at Brenda's formidable cleavage during each of their sessions. After learning about how to be a good Catholic couple, they were married in a simple, sensible ceremony.

Standing at the altar, looking down at Brenda's hands, Bert noticed, perhaps for the first time, how long her fingers were, the tiny bump just above the first knuckle on the middle finger of her left hand, and how cold her fingertips felt pressed against his. In that moment, he believed and vowed, in front of God and the small congregation of loved ones, that their marriage would endure, that their love would endure because Brenda looked so beautiful. He was touched by the way her hand trembled slightly as he slid her wedding ring on her finger. He saw the tears at the corners of her eyes. He felt the pounding of his own heart, in that time when it was secured in the meat of his chest, warm, pulsing, alive. Truly understanding his heart for the first time, Bert mistook the nervous pounding for nothing less than passion for the woman standing across from him. During their honeymoon in Niagara Falls, however, when Brenda demanded they leave the city after Bert graduated, he realized he knew nothing about his new wife and his new wife knew nothing about him. It was a disappointment. From then on, his heart beat a little slower, became a little less moored, until it dislodged completely.

I should have never left New York, Bert thought, not for the first time, as he stared at his dream-house plans, two months after meeting with his divorce attorney. But then he decided not to dwell on the life that might have, should have been and leaned back in his chair, turning in a slow circle. He was going to build his house. He had always planned to build it for Brenda, a monument to their marriage, but he now realized that, if he had done that, the house would have crumbled to its foundation the moment she stepped across the threshold. He didn't know whom he was building it for now, but it was going to be the one right thing he did with his life. Just looking at the strong, upward lines of the exterior facade made him shiver.

When he looked up, he saw Alicia staring at him. She smiled, an unfamiliar kindness in her eyes, and Bert knew in that moment they were closer than they had ever been. Just as quickly she disappeared. Bert felt a slight burning in his chest. He couldn't breathe when she was around. He opened the top desk drawer and fumbled for his inhaler, taking a long puff, then headed down the street to his lawyer's office, a jaunt in his step as he thought of his former mistress draped in his doorway and across his body at their favorite hotel, where he tried to make the building move from the inside with the force of every thrust.

The lawyer looked more pregnant than ever. She was mocking him with her fertility, with her tumescent belly and scrubbed, healthy glow. He could hear a loud, high-pitched ringing and he clenched his eyes shut until it went away. When he opened his eyes again, Ursula was staring at him curiously.

"Are you okay?" she asked.

"What does Brenda want?"

"She's going after the land."

I will not cry in front of a woman, Bert told himself. *I will be a stoic man.* "That's the only thing I want. This is not at all fair."

"Divorce isn't fair."

"What's it going to cost me to keep the land?"

"Half of its current value."

Bert did some quick mental calculations and nodded.

Ursula rubbed her forehead, groaning loudly, her face paling. "You're the boss," she said softly, rubbing her stomach.

Bert cocked his head to the side. "Are you okay?"

Ursula tried to stand. "I think I'm having a contraction."

Bert's pulse quickened. He felt slightly nauseated. Fertility was not only mocking him; it was stalking him. "Shouldn't we call someone?"

Ursula grimaced. "Can you help me up?"

Bert rushed out of his seat and around the desk. Sliding one arm around the lawyer's waist, he hoisted her to her feet. There was a light splashing sound, and soon they were

standing in a small, murky pool of something Bert wanted no part of. *I am standing in a pool of fertility*, he thought. *I am cursed.*

Ursula's face turned crimson. "My water just broke."

"Don't panic," Bert said. "I've seen this in the movies. I know what to do." He stretched his arm, resting his trembling hand just above Ursula's navel, at the most swollen part of her belly. He felt something, though he didn't know what, and for a moment he forgot where he was. He felt a great weight pushing his shoulders down until he was belly to eye with the great mass about to give way. The loud ringing came back, and Bert couldn't help himself. He brushed his lips across his lawyer's stomach and then, mercifully, the ringing went away.

Ursula pushed him away. "What are you doing?"

"I'm sorry," Bert stuttered. "I don't know what came over me."

Ursula wiped her forehead. "Can you tell my secretary to call my husband?"

Bert nodded and hastily backed out of the office. Seconds later, he watched Ursula begin a quick waddle out of the building and ran after her. "Wait. Is there something I can do to help? Give you a ride or something?"

Ursula stopped, then turned around and grunted, hunching over. "I'm fine. I wouldn't want something to come over you again."

Bert shook his head. "It wouldn't feel right to let you go to the hospital by yourself. I'll just drop you off. "

"No," Ursula called after him weakly, but she sat on a bench in front of the building, watching as Bert ran the few blocks to his office, where his car was parked.

Bert could feel his lungs tightening in protest, but he ignored the discomfort, didn't even stop to find relief from his inhaler. Minutes later, they were on the way to the hospital, Ursula talking to her husband on Bert's cell phone.

Bert loosened his grip on the steering wheel. "Your husband is nervous?"

She nodded, breathing in short, tense spurts. "Our first child."

They were silent for the rest of the ride, and Bert couldn't help but smile as he saw a boy as young and eager as his partner Todd standing by the emergency room doors.

"There's Solomon," Ursula said. "Prompt as ever." She turned to look at Bert. "He's the responsible one in our marriage."

The lawyer's husband opened his wife's door and helped her out of the car, then reached across the passenger seat, vigorously shaking Bert's hand, thanking him profusely with those Midwestern manners Bert still found so charming.

"Is there anything else I can do?" Bert asked.

Ursula grunted, holding her stomach. "I've got it from here. I'll be in touch about the case."

Bert stood in front of the hospital and thought about breathing—simple for most people, difficult for asthmatics and pregnant women. There was an irony in there somewhere.

A few months later, he sat on a pile of concrete blocks on the construction site of his new house. The foundation had been laid, the framework erected, and the space was silent as the sun began to set. He could already imagine walking across the wooden floors, corking open a bottle of wine in the backyard, sharing the space with a woman he had yet to meet or perhaps a woman he had once known, like Alicia, who still smiled at him from the doorway of his office with intriguing frequency. It felt good to indulge in such flights of fancy. Brenda was probably cursing him as she contemplated the mere possibility of his happiness. That also felt good. Reaching into his coat pocket, Bert pulled out a thank-you card from his lawyer. *It's a boy!!!*, she wrote, thanking him for the ride and assuring him that he was in good hands with the colleague who would be handling the divorce now that she was on maternity leave. A picture of a fat, pink baby boy sucking on his small fist fell out of the envelope. For reasons he could not explain even to himself, Bert cried for the third time in his life. Staring past the picture of this lawyer's child, he saw the wooden skeleton of his new home swaying back and forth.

Chapter 5

CARGO PLANE

–

Jonathan Safran Foer

'm writing this from the Genius Bar of the Mac Store—the epicenter of the opposite of genius. I was un-genius enough to erase a folder I was un-genius enough to name "Documents," which contained more or less everything I've written since I became literate.

The last time I did something like this was about a decade ago. I had a good friend—no longer a friend, sadly—whose family owned the largest and most diabolical security firm in the world. They were the guys who recovered the data from Saddam Hussein's computers. So they were good enough for me.

I dropped off my laptop, and a week later was given a stack of about 200 CD-ROMS, or whatever they were then called.

"What's on these?" I asked.

"Everything," I was told.

Everything is usually an overstatement, but in this case there should have been a more impressive word. Not only did the discs contain every file I'd ever written, and every draft of every file I'd ever written, but a still of every screen I'd ever looked at: Google searches, Amazon purchases, eBay browsing, e-mails in progress, thousands of front pages of the *New York Times*.... If that had been everything, it would have been an awesome everything. But there was more. Image after image after image I had never seen before: I remember a black-and-white photo of Paul Celan's deep purple eyes and the road map of a town on the Costa Brava; I remember the brickwork of Alvar Aalto's "Experimental House" and tangled parachutes; I remember the hands of the Swedish rug designer Märta Måås-Fjetterström (identified by the caption: "Märta Måås-Fjetterström, weaver of dreams")....

I *hadn't* ever seen those things, but *could* have. It was a slide show of a possible life, or of my dream life, or subconscious. (Or, as it turned out, of my future life.) I thought about making a book of those images; it would have required a spine as wide as you are tall.

Two summers later, I went to that town—Cadaqués. And Aalto's house, which I still long to visit, is my favorite building in the world. And the first thing I bought for my post-divorce home was a Märta Måås-Fjetterström rug. Maybe you could make sense of the tangled parachutes.

How does one explain unjustified knowledge? My first thought upon having sex for the first time was, "This is exactly as I'd dreamt it." I didn't mean emotionally, but physically. I knew what it would feel like before I felt it. Not approximately, not nearly, but exactly. The knowledge had been coiled within me, in much the same way that the knowledge of feeding is coiled within newborns.

One of my favorite albums is *Beauty Is a Rare Thing*—a compilation of Ornette Coleman's recordings with Atlantic Records. (I know almost nothing about jazz, but was given it as a present from someone I used to be close with.) Coleman played a plastic saxophone, because it sounded unlike the brass instrument everyone else played. And he played his strange instrument strangely—very strangely, very much on purpose. He played it so strangely that he was one of the greatest musicians of the 20th century.

And so strangely that this happened: touring the South, in the early '50s, he was pulled over by a racist cop, who accused him of having stolen the saxophone that was resting on the passenger seat. Coleman protested, explained that he was performing at a major concert hall that night, that he had recorded more than a dozen albums, and so on. The cop shoved the saxophone into Coleman's hands and said, "Play it and prove it." Coleman played it, but proved something different. He played his strange instrument in his strange way—and the cop confiscated the saxophone, having had his suspicion, he thought, confirmed.

The thing is, Coleman was fully capable of playing any piece of music ever written, in any style he chose. He could just as easily—far more easily—have blown the cop away with a prodigious, if typical, rendition of a standard.

Why didn't he? Why didn't he just play a pretty song and get on with life?

Why do some people find it impossible to just get on with life?

Here's a passage from a John Ashbery essay, about avant-garde art, that I often find myself thinking about. (He's referring to American avant-garde artists in the middle of the 20th century.)

To experiment was to have the feeling that one was poised on some outermost brink. In other words, if one wanted to depart, even moderately, from the norm, one was taking one's life—one's life as an artist—into one's hands. A painter like Pollock,

*for instance, was gambling everything on the fact
that he was the greatest painter in America, for if
he wasn't, he was nothing, and the drips would
turn out to be random splashes from the brush of a
careless housepainter. It must often have occurred
to Pollock that there was just a possibility that he
wasn't an artist at all, that he had spent his life
"toiling up the wrong road to art," as Flaubert said
to Zola. But this very real possibility is paradoxi-
cally just what makes the tremendous excitement in
his work. It is a gamble against terrific odds. Most
reckless things are beautiful in some way, and reck-
lessness is what makes experimental art beautiful,
just as religions are beautiful because of the strong
possibility that they are founded on nothing. We
would all believe in God if we knew He existed, but
would this be much fun?*

Nope. And it wouldn't be belief, either.

I love that sentence: "Most reckless things are beautiful in some way."

I also love: "the outermost brink."

In the months after my divorce, I would wake up in
the middle of every night and watch a documentary. This
habit became a ritual, and there were no exceptions. I
learned about the honeybee apocalypse. I learned about
the last hunters and gatherers, and the Large Hadron
Collider. I learned about the deadliest day on Everest,
avant-garde Spanish cuisine, the organized resistance to

light pollution, Nina Simone, Magnus Carlsen, Charles and Ray Eames, Edward Snowden, the battle for the soul of contemporary origami....

I also became enamored of lists: facts, untranslatable words from other languages, details. I liked—I suddenly *needed*—to know how things worked: I interrogated locksmiths and pilots and greenmarket farmers. I read books with titles like *How Architecture Functions* and *The Anatomy of a City*. I rewired a functioning chandelier. I snaked an unclogged toilet. I asked the phone company to install a second line—despite never using the primary one—so that I could watch it done.

- *Days are longer than years on Mercury. On Mercury, you have multiple birthdays on your birthday.*

- *Tsundoku* (Japanese): Leaving a book unread after buying it.

- *Some snails can sleep for three years.*

- *Mokita* (Papua New Guinean): The truth everyone knows, but agrees not to talk about.

- *Astronauts see up to sixteen sunrises and sunsets every day.*

- *Fernweh* (German): Feeling homesick for a place you have never been.

- *There are, at any given time, forty times in the world.*

- *Tingo* (Pascuense): To gradually steal all the possessions out of a neighbor's house by borrowing and not returning.

- *Astronauts' footprints stay on the moon forever; there's no wind to blow them away.*

- *Jayus* (Indonesian): An unfunny joke told so poorly that it is funny.

- *Cleopatra lived closer in time to the moon landing than the construction of the Great Pyramid of Giza.*

- *A ventriloquist invented the artificial heart.*

- *Mamihlapinatapei* (Yagan): The wordless, meaningful look shared by two people who both desire to initiate something, but are both reluctant to do so.

- *Only 66 years separate the Wright Brothers' flight and the moon landing.*

- *Ventriloquism used to be hugely popular on the radio.*

- *Culaccino* (Italian): The mark left on a table by a moist glass.

- *Torschlusspanik* (German): The fear of diminishing opportunities as one ages.

- *There is a cemetery for dummies whose human partners have died.*

- *Iktsuarpok* (Inuit): The feeling of anticipation that leads you to keep looking outside to see if a special person is coming.

- *There are more people alive now than have died in all of human history.*

- *Cafuné* (Portuguese): Tenderly running one's fingers

through someone's hair.

- *Ten percent of all photos ever taken were taken in the last year.*

- *The oldest human footprint found on earth is 350,000 years old.*

- *Neil Armstrong left his space boots on the moon, in order to compensate for the weight of the moon rocks he brought back with him.*

- *Ya'aburnee* (Arabic): A declaration of hope to die before another person.

- *As there is no wind in space, they had to put metal mesh in the American flag that was planted on the moon so that it would stay open.*

- *A space shuttle weighs about 220,000 pounds.*

- *Komorebi* (Japanese): The sunlight that filters through the leaves of the trees.

- *Autumn leaves can be seen from space.*

- *Six million pounds of space dust settle on the earth every year.*

- *Tartle* (Scottish): Hesitating while introducing someone, because you've forgotten their name.

- *There are nighttime rainbows. They are called moonbows.*

- *No one knows what color dinosaurs were. Green is a guess.*

- *The astronauts of the Challenger disaster probably*

didn't die until they hit the water; at least three of the seven turned on their emergency oxygen supply after the explosion.

- *A snowflake can take two hours to fall from a cloud to the ground.*

- *The brontosaurus never existed. It was a mistaken combination of the head of one kind of dinosaur and the body of another.*

- *Parachutes were invented before airplanes.*

- *The famous death matches between the two most famous dinosaurs, the* Tyrannosaurus rex *and the stegosaurus, never happened. They existed almost one hundred million years apart. There is more time between the T. rex and stegosaurus than between the T. rex and humans.*

- *Hanyauku* (Rukwangali): Walking on tiptoes across warm sand.

- *The average dream lasts about 20 minutes. There is a misconception that dreams feel much longer than they are. In most cases, they usually feel much shorter than they are.*

I don't know how long the months after my divorce lasted. Months is a guess. One night I didn't wake up until morning, and after that I never watched another documentary.

Have you ever come across the word "esquivalience?" It's a made-up word—a "ghost word"—in the *New Oxford American Dictionary*, created to detect breaches of copyright. (There would be no other way to know if another dictionary-maker had simply stolen Oxford's list of words; ghost words prove plagiarism.) For the same reason, encyclopedias of music often include a piece of nonexistent music, and mathematic tables often contain nonexistent equations, and, hauntingly, most atlases map at least one fictitious place. They're known as "paper towns," or "phantom settlements".

There was a phantom settlement in upstate New York (in old Esso maps) called Agloe. But it lost its phantom status in the 1950s when someone, believing himself to be in Agloe, opened the Agloe General Store there, and it became a real place. The store closed, but the place persisted. It was included in other atlases, and continued to exist until the 1990s, at which point it disappeared again. But it didn't disappear to the same non-existence. It's more like a person—the death after life is different than the death before being born.

Esquivalience is defined as "the willful avoidance of one's official responsibilities."

It's nice to imagine being esquivalient—maybe even living in one's own phantom settlement, speaking only ghost words over nonexistent music—while at the same time utterly
responsible and devoted to all of the things one loves. That would be something.

One day I'll tell you the fullest version of this story, which ended up changing my life in some dramatic and concrete ways, but this will do for now: about two years ago, I went to Chicago—where I'm from—to visit the dying mother of my oldest friend. She used to carry me down the stairs of nursery school when I'd become panicked at the top. (Humans aren't born with a fear of heights, by the way, they learn it.) Thirty years later, I was panicked about going to see her—being at the top of death's stairs—but it was my turn to carry her. It wasn't the proximity to death that I was afraid of, but that I might accidentally say too much, or too little. To protect against awkward silences, I brought a small stack of poems to read. That afternoon was one of the least awkward of my life, but I did end up reading her the poems, and rereading them.

At the bottom of this e-mail is one of the poems I read to her. It's by the Russian poet Joseph Brodsky. That line—"I wish I knew no astronomy when stars appear"—is one way to summarize all that we've exchanged thus far.

Brodsky was put on trial when he was 24, and ultimately sent to a labor camp in Siberia. His case turned him into a symbol of artistic resistance, and a hero to poets everywhere. (He won the Nobel Prize in 1987.) Here are just a few lines from the transcript:

JUDGE: What is your specific occupation?
BRODSKY: Poet.
JUDGE: And who said you're a poet? Who ranked you among poets?
BRODSKY: No one. Who ranked me as a member of the human race?

I visited Brodsky's grave on San Michele, an island in the Venetian lagoon. Rather than flowers, or pebbles, or notes, people leave pens for him. For one another. I don't remember the image of a grave covered in pens among the hundreds of thousands of "recovered" files, but then it would have required my life to go through all of those images, and I also wanted to live.

There are things that I've always known and then have had confirmed—my experience with sex. But there are also things that I've always known, but haven't yet had proven. An unbearably embarrassing example is my recurrent dream of flying. I feel that I know exactly what it would be like to fly. I'll never know if I'm right to believe what I believe, but I am sure of what I am sure of. In most cases, such unexperienced knowledge doesn't really matter. (I'm not about to jump from the top of a flight of stairs.) In some cases, it requires what, in your last e-mail, you called "a rearrangement of self." Sometimes, knowledge of the outermost brink forbids us from just playing a pretty song and getting on with life.

I am beyond the months after, but still occasionally seek information. I learned a great fact this morning, browsing on one of the new Macs while waiting for my appointment at the Genius Bar: The entire Wright Brothers' flight could be contained in the belly of the kind of cargo plane that transports the Space Shuttle on its back. Imagine that: a cargo plane flying with a space traveler on its back, and the first flight in its belly.

Inside of the cargo plane of this letter is the simple response I'd intended to write. But there's also an interstellar voyager above it.

Blame it on my *iktsuarpok.*

CHURCH AND STATE OF MIND

–

Sloane Crosley

When it comes to workplaces, the personal and the professional have always had a way of overlapping. You put a bunch of people who share fundamental interests in the same room for eight hours a day, five days a week, and what do you think is going to happen? Over the years, sitcoms have trained us to believe there is one major route the personal takes through the professional, and that route is the love story—Sam and Diane, Jim and Pam, Roger and Joan. But in real life, in modern life, professional-turned-personal relationships are more varied. They lean toward the legitimately complicated over the adorably awkward. They also tend to last more than half an hour. It was therefore refreshing to read the lyrics to Aimee Mann and Jonathan Coulton's "Lost in the Cloud":

> Access code accepted
> I'm announcing my name
> She's a disembodied voice and I am the same

The song has Mann's trademark combination of warmth and distance, painting a portrait of longing and isolation brought on by an unrequited office crush. A man or woman has decided to work from home but still has to have a conference call with the object of his or her affection, a person who, come Monday, will be "nothing but nice/Ask me how my weekend was/ She'll probably ask twice." Like the previous chapters, the song provides a contrast in spaces—work is a place of printers, home is a place of eating peanut butter from the jar— but it is ultimately a song about the delicate balance of maintaining a personal relationship with someone with whom you have a professional relationship. If you're not careful, you can lose both.

Joyce Carol Oates's "The Happy Place" also walks that fine line. A creative-writing professor at an elite American university becomes intrigued by a student named Ana, "who holds herself apart from the others." Ana is quiet and reserved, and yet the professor senses a deep well of emotion in her and, in the words of E. M. Forster, would like only to connect. She means it literally. "You feel an impulse to lean across the table, to touch Ana's wrist. To smile at her, ask—'Ana, is something wrong?'" The professor misses Ana when she's not there. She feels she must protect her student but is also conflicted about the feeling, wondering about Ana's life

beyond the classroom. Eventually, the profes-
sor does get Ana to tap into her own creative
vein. But once tapped, the flow of that vein looks
nothing like she expected it to.

Chapter 6

LOST IN THE CLOUD
(TODAY I WORK FROM HOME)
–
Aimee Mann & Jonathan Coulton

Access code accepted, I'm announcing my name
She's a disembodied voice, and I am the same
I hear the thrumming and hissing of space
My small talk dies in the crowd
She speaks, I picture her face
But I keep breaking up
And the pieces get lost in the cloud

Office clock on a kitchen wall
A steady metronome
I don't want to go in at all
Today I work from home

There are no distractions when
You go it alone
Private conversations
Overheard on the phone
I make a sandwich and eat by the sink
Here I don't have to be proud
Just need a minute to think
But the wires get crossed
And I'm suddenly lost in the cloud

Tried to Skype with the background clutter
Printer, mug, and comb
Worker bee eating peanut butter
Today I work from home

I was a fool, what a fool,
And I knew that I was
Saying, Cool, it's cool, it's cool
She can do what she does

If I'm in on Monday she'll
Be nothing but nice
Ask me how my weekend was
She'll probably ask twice
You have to walk such a delicate line
Where hoping isn't allowed
Those hopes, those pictures were mine
File not found
Everything lost in the cloud

Back and forth but it's all the same
I know this palindrome
All the letters will spell your name
Today I work from home

Lost In The Cloud
(Today I Work From Home)

Chapter 7

THE HAPPY PLACE

-

Joyce Carol Oates

P*rofessor! Hello.*

White winter days, sunshine on newly fallen snow.

You have come to the *happy place* for it is Thursday afternoon.

Another week, and you are still alive. Your secret you carry everywhere and so into the *happy place*.

So close to the heart, no one will see.

*

Not a happy season. Not a happy time. Not in the history of the world and not in the personal lives of many.

You wonder how many are like you. Having come to prefer dark to daylight. Sweet oblivion of sleep to raw wakefulness.

Yet: in the wood-paneled seminar room on the fifth floor of North Hall. At the top of the smooth-worn wooden staircase where a leaded window overlooks a stand of juniper pines. In the wind, pine boughs shiver and flash with melting snow. The *happy place*.

Here is an atmosphere of optimism light as helium. You laugh often, you and the undergraduates spaced about the polished table.

Why do you laugh so much?—you have wondered.

Generally it seems: the more serious the subjects, the more likely some sort of laughter.

The more intensity, the more laughter.

The more at stake, the more laughter.

The *happy place* is the solace. The promise.

Waking in the morning stunned to be *still alive*. The profound fact of your life now.

*

Already, at the first class meeting in September, you'd noticed her: *Ana.*

Of the twelve students in the fiction writing workshop, it is *Ana* who holds herself apart from the others. From you.

When they laugh, Ana does not laugh—not often.

When they answer questions you put to them, when in their enthusiasm they talk over one another like puppies tumbling together—Ana sits silent. Though Ana may look on with a faint (melancholy) smile.

Or, Ana may turn her gaze toward the wall of windows casting a ghostly reflected light onto her face and seem to be staring into space—oblivious of her surroundings.

Thinking her own thoughts. Private, not yours to know.

You feel an impulse to lean across the table, to touch Ana's wrist. To smile at her, ask—*Ana, is something wrong?*

But what would you dare ask this girl who holds herself apart from her classmates? *Are you troubled? Unhappy? Distracted? Bored?*—not possible. One of the others in the seminar might take Ana aside to ask such questions, but you, the adult in the room, the Professor, don't have that right, nor would you exercise that right if indeed it were yours. Still less should you touch Ana's wrist.

It is a very thin wrist. The wrist of a child. So easily snapped! The young woman's face is delicately boned, pale, smooth as porcelain, her eyes are beautiful and thick-lashed but somewhat shadowed, evasive.

You have noticed, around Ana's slender neck, a thin gold chain with a small gold cross.

The little cross must be positioned just so, in the hollow at the base of Ana's throat that is as pronounced and (once you have noticed it) conspicuous as your own.

(What is it called?—*suprasternal notch*. A physical feature aligned with thinness, generally conceded to be a genetic inheritance.)

Indeed, Ana is a very diminutive young woman. To the casual eye, she would seem more likely fourteen than eighteen and hardly a *woman* at all.

Ana must weigh less than one hundred pounds. No more than five feet two. You see, without having actually noticed until now, that she wears loose-fitting clothing, a shapeless pullover several sizes too large, and the thought strikes you, unbidden, fleeting, that Ana may be acutely *thin*. Her diffident manner makes her appear even smaller. *As if she might curl up, disappear. Cast no shadow.*

How vulnerable Ana appears!—to gaze upon her is to feel that you must protect her.

Yet, you suppose that there are many who would wish to take advantage of her.

When the others speak of "religious belief"— "superstition"—with the heedlessness of bright adolescents wielding their wits like blades, Ana sits very still at her end of the table, eyes downcast. Touching the cross around her neck.

Why doesn't Ana speak, intervene? Defend her beliefs, if indeed she has beliefs?

Yes. This is a superstitious symbol I am wearing. What is it to you?

The discussion has risen out of the week's assignment, a short story by Flannery O'Connor saturated with Christian imagery and the mystery of the Eucharist, and Ana, like the others, has written an analysis of the story.

But Ana remains silent, stiff until at last the discussion veers in another direction. Glancing at you, an expression of—is it reproach? hurt?—for just an instant.

*

The *insomniac night* is the antithesis of the *happy place*.

Unlike the *happy place*, which is specifically set, and unfortunately finite, as an academic class invariably comes to an end, the *insomniac night* has no natural end.

If you cannot sleep in the night, the night will simply continue into the next, sun-blinding day.

*

You have thought, *Is she a refugee,* for her spoken English is hesitant, imperfect. You have not wanted to think, *Is she a victim. Has she been hurt. What is the sorrow in her face. Why is she so unlike the others.*

Ana's face, that seems wise beyond her years. (You are certain you are not misinterpreting.)

Oh, why does Ana not *smile*? Why is it Ana who alone resists the *happy place*?

In 27 years of teaching you have encountered a number of *Anas*—surely.

Yet, you don't recall. Not one. And why should you, students are impermanent in the lives of teachers. There is nothing profound in this situation. Ana has done adequate work for the course, she has never failed to hand in her work on time. You have no reason to ask her to come and speak with you, no reason at all.

Ana's reluctance (refusal?) to smile on cue, as others so easily smile—this is a small mystery.

Is it your pride that is hurt? But how little pride means to you, frankly.

You are conscious of the (unwitting) tyranny of the group. Of any group, no matter how congenial, well-intentioned.

That all in the group laugh, smile, agree with the others, or "disagree" politely, or flirtatiously. The (unwitting) tyranny of the classroom that even the most liberal-minded instructor cannot fail to exert. Pay attention to me. *Pay attention to the forward motion of the class. No silences! No inward turning—this is not a Zen meditation. A small class is a sort of skiff, we are all paddling. We are all responsible for paddling. We are aiming for the same destination. We are aware (some of us keenly) of those who are not paddling. Those who have set their paddles aside.*

Perhaps Ana has not clearly understood that enrollment in a small seminar brings with it a degree of responsibility for participation. Answering questions, asking questions. "Discussing." The workshop is not a lecture course: students are not expected to take notes. Perhaps it was an error in judgment for Ana to enroll in a course in which (it seems apparent) she has so little interest as, you are thinking, it was an error in judgment for you to accept her application, out of 70 applications for a workshop of twelve.

Why had you chosen Ana Fallas? A first-year student, with no background in creative writing? Something in the writing sample Ana had provided must have appealed to you, a glimpse of Hispanic domestic life perhaps, that set it aside from others that were merely good, conventional.

Though now, as it has turned out, Ana's work has seemed less exceptional. Careful, circumspect. Nothing grammatically wrong but—nothing to call attention to itself.

As if Ana is trying to make herself into one of *them*— the Caucasian majority.

It is likely that Ana is intimidated by the university— its size, its reputation. By the other students in the writing class. She is but one of only two first-year students, and the other is Shan from Beijing, a dazzling prodigy intending to major in neuroscience.

The others are older than Ana, more experienced. Three are seniors, immersed in original research—senior theses. Most of them are Americans and those who are not, like Shan, and Ansar (Pakistan), and Colin (UK), have studied in the United States previously and seem to have traveled widely. Ana is the only Hispanic student in the class and (you are guessing) she might be the first in her family to have enrolled in college.

Is Ana aware of you, your concern for her? Sometimes you think *yes*. More often you think *no. Not at all.*

*

I can't.

Or, *I don't think that I can…*

At the age of 22, you were terrified at the prospect of teaching your first class.

English Composition. A large urban university. An evening class.

More than a quarter-century ago and yet—vivid in memory!

You had never taught before. You had a master's degree in English but had never been (like most of your graduate student friends, and your husband) a teaching assistant. Amazing to you now, that the chairman of an English Department in a quite reputable private university had hired you to teach, though you'd had no experience teaching at all—had not once stood in front of a classroom. (He'd said afterward that he had been impressed by the written work of yours he'd seen, in national publications. He'd said that, in his experience, teaching was best picked up *on the fly*, like learning to ride a bicycle, or like sex.)

It had been thrilling to you, to be selected over numerous others with experience, older than you. But it had not been so thrilling to contemplate the actual teaching. At 22, you would not be much older, in fact you would be younger, than many of your students enrolled in the university's night school division.

English composition! The most commonly taught of university courses, along with remedial English and math.

Your husband, young himself at the time, just 30, had tried to dispel your terror. He'd tried to encourage you, tease you. Saying—*Don't be afraid, I can walk you into the classroom on my shoes.*

Such a silly notion, you'd laughed. Tears of apprehension in your eyes and yet you'd laughed. Your husband had that power, to calm you.

Between your young husband and you, in those years. Much laughter.

You think you will live forever. Always it will be like this. You don't think—well, you don't think.

Your husband had a PhD in English. He was an assistant professor at another, nearby university, he'd been a very successful teacher for several years. Gently he reasoned with you: what could possibly go wrong, once you'd prepared for the first class?

What could go wrong? Everything!

They won't pay attention to me. They will see that I am too young—inexperienced. They will laugh in derision. Some of them will walk out....

Your husband convinced you that such fears were groundless. Ridiculous. University students would not walk out of a class. Especially older students would not walk out of a class for which they'd paid tuition—it was a serious business to them, not a lark.

In this class, so long ago, were 30 students. Thirty! Over-large for a composition class.

To you, 30 strangers. You broke into an actual sweat, contemplating them. The prospect of entering the classroom was dazzling. A nightmare.

For days beforehand, you rehearsed your first words—
Hello! This is English one-oh-one and my name is—which
you hoped would not be stammered, and would be audible.
For days you pondered—what should you wear?

On that crucial evening, your husband drove you to the
university. Your husband did not *walk you into the room
on his shoes*, but he did accompany you to the assigned
classroom in the ground floor of an old red-brick building.
(Did your husband kiss you, for good luck? A brush of his
lips on your cheek?) How breathless you were by this time,
seeing your prospective students pass you oblivious of you.

Wish me luck.

I love you!

And so it happened, when you stepped into the classroom, and took your place behind a podium in front of a
blackboard, and introduced yourself to rows of strangers
gazing at you with the most rapt interest you'd ever drawn
from any strangers in your life—an unexpected and astonishing conviction flooded over you, of *happiness*.

Knowing you were in the right place, at just the right
time.

*

You feel her absence keenly.

This day, a particularly wet, cold day, Ana is absent
from the workshop.

Reluctant to begin class, you wait for several minutes.
(For other students are arriving late.) Then, when it is
evident that Ana will not be coming, you begin.

You have noticed that Ana sits in the same place at the table each week. She will arrive early, to assure this. Such (rigid?) behavior is the sign of a shy person; a person who has had enough upset in her life, and now wants a predictable routine; a person who chooses to rein in her emotions; a person who knows that, like internal hemorrhaging, emotions are not infinite, and can be fatal.

Tacitly, the others have conceded Ana's place at the (farther) end of the table. No one would take Ana's chair, just as no one would take the professor's usual seat.

Yet, no one mentions Ana's absence. So little impression has she made on the class, no one thinks to wonder aloud—*Hey, where is Ana?*

You ask for a volunteer, to provide Ana with the assignment for the following week. At first, no one responds. Then, a young woman raises her hand—*Sure! She's in my residence hall, I think.*

You might email or text Ana yourself. But you are thinking you would like someone from the workshop to volunteer, to forge a connection with Ana, however slight.

*

That evening, Ana sends you an email, apologizing for her absence.

Flu, infirmary sorry to miss class. Will make up missing work.

*

Ridiculous, you are *so relieved.*

Smiling, your heart suffused with—what? Hope like a helium-filled balloon.

When Ana returns to the workshop you tell her—*We missed you, Ana.*

True, to a degree. *You* missed her.

Naturally, Ana has completed the assignment: the reading in the anthology, and the weekly prose piece. Though Ana is not one of the more imaginative writers, Ana is the most diligent of students.

Hers has been good work, acceptable work so far this semester. It is careful work, precisely written English, surprisingly free of errors for one whose speech is uncertain. Is this the utterance of clenched jaws?—you wonder. Maybe Ana would like to scream.

You will encourage her to write more freely. From the heart.

You will tell her—in fact, you will tell the class— *Write what feels like life to you. It need not be "true"—your writing will make it "true."*

Ana frowns distractedly, staring down at the table. She knows that you are (obliquely) criticizing her work, which the others have discussed politely, without much to say about it. For all her pose of indifference, Ana is highly sensitive.

You have encouraged your students to write, not memoir, but *memoir-like* fiction. You do not (truly!) want these young people to open their veins and pour out their life's blood for the diversion of others, but neither do you want them to attempt arch, artificial fiction derivative of work by the most-read fiction writers of the era—for that they cannot do, and certainly they cannot do well.

Others in the class take up the challenge, excited. *Write what feels like life to you.*

Ana takes back her prose piece from you. Ana's eyes slide away from yours and will not engage.

You had written—*Promising! But something that anyone might have written. What does "Ana" have to say?*

Away from the seminar room, which is the *happy place*, you ponder your obsession with this student. For the first time, acknowledging the word—*obsession.*

Telling yourself that now you've made the acknowledgment, the *obsession* will begin to fade.

*

And then, in the seventh week of the semester, long past the time when you'd have thought that any undergraduate could surprise you, Ana hands in something very different from the cautious prose she has been writing.

The assignment is a dramatic monologue. Just a page or two. In the "memoirist" mode.

Here is urgent, intense work by Ana. Not cautious at all—a bold plunge into stream-of-consciousness speech uttered (seemingly) by an adolescent daughter of (Guatemalan?) (illegal?) immigrants stranded in a nightmare detention center at the Texas border in Laredo.

The other young writers take notice. It is requested

that Ana read the monologue aloud.

Oh, I—I can't....

Stammering *no*, blushing fiercely, but the others insist.

*

From a prose poem of Ana's: *I thought the eucalyptus had burst into flame, I'd seen it and ran away screaming. And then—years later they laugh at me and told me no, that had not happened to me but to my little sister.*

And when I remember my brother beaten by our father with his fists they tell me no, not just my brother but me, as well. But they are not laughing.

In the foster home there are three girls named Mya.

Those acts perpetrated upon one of the Myas are perpetrated upon the others.

We do not know your name but your face will always be known to us.

*

Astonishing and wonderful—Ana is writing with such passion now.

Less guardedly, and less circumspectly. Wonderful too, how others in the seminar take up her work with excitement and admiration.

This is not conventional "fiction"—there are few "characters"—minimal "description"—"settings." All is dreamlike, rapid-fire.

In fragments, it is revealed that a girl named "Mya"

has lived in one or more foster homes in the Southwest. Albuquerque, Tucson. In the home are (illegal?) Central American immigrants. There are bribes to be paid. There are hopes for visas, green cards. There are knives, guns. Brutal beatings when debts are not repaid. Shootings, woundings, blood-soaked mattresses. A ghastly scene in an emergency room where an eighteen-year-old Guatemalan hemorrhages to death, and a laconic scene in a morgue in which a drug-addled woman attempts to identify an estranged and badly mutilated husband. Hiding from law enforcement officers, rummaging dumpsters for food. Shoplifting. Unexpected cruelty in the foster home, and unexpected kindness.

Homeless children, adolescents. A girl seeking out a younger sister who has been sent to live in a foster home.

There was no choice. My mother believed our father would kill her if she did not leave.

...first there were three Myas in the foster home. Then there were two Myas. Then there was one Mya.

Then, none.

*

You are filled with dread, you have gone too far. Your shy, unassertive student has begun writing *what feels like life—* she has thrown off restraint.

It is true, you have triumphed—as a writing instructor. But this is a precarious triumph—(maybe). As if you have prized open a shell, the pulsing life of the defenseless mollusk within is exposed.

One of the most imaginative writers in the class, whose

name is Philip, whose major is astrophysics and whose favored writers are Borges, Calvino, Cortázar, declares that Ana's prose poetry is *beautiful and terrible as a Mobius strip.*

Ana is deeply moved to hear these words. You have seen how Philip has been casting sidelong glances at Ana over the weeks; now, Ana lifts her eyes to his face.

Much attention is paid in the workshop to Ana's prose. Her sentences, paragraphs—headlong plunges of language. There is praise for Ana's spare, elliptical dialogue which is buried in the text as if it might be interior and not uttered aloud at all.

No one cares to address Ana's powerful subject matter. Desperate persons, domestic violence, a hint of sexual assault. *Three girls named Mya in the foster home.*

Amid their admiration, the others are uneasy. It is considered bad manners—the violation of an implicit taboo—to ask if anyone's work is based upon her experiences, at least when the work is so extreme. And you have taken care to instruct the students, memoirist writing is *not memoir.* Even memoir is not "autobiography" but understood to be more poetic and impressionistic, less literal and complete.

At the end of the discussion, Ana is flushed with pleasure. Unless it's an excited sort of dread. Never have you seen Ana so intense, so involved in the workshop.

You would not dare reach out to touch her wrist now, her burning-hot skin would scald your fingers.

*

The following Thursday, Ana is not in the seminar room when you arrive.

Everyone waits for Ana's arrival. The chair in which she usually sits is left unoccupied. But she does not appear.

Your heart is seized with dismay. You are sure it's as you'd feared—Ana regrets what she revealed to the class, she regrets being led to such openness.

Having written what she has written, that cannot now be retracted.

I am so sorry, Ana. Forgive me.

You don't write such an email. Never!

From your husband, you learned never to impose your emotions upon students. Never to assume to know what they are thinking and feeling, that is (but) what you imagine they are thinking and feeling, unless they tell you; and it would be rare indeed for them to tell you.

You are the adult. You are the professional. You must prevail.

*

And then: by chance, you encounter Ana in a store near the university.

Indeed it is but *by chance*. Indeed, *you have not been following Ana.*

Seeing too, another time—how alone Ana appears. How small, vulnerable.

Inside an oversized winter coat falling nearly to her

ankles, that looks like a hand-me-down.

Her face is flushed from the cold, her eyes startled and damp. Faint shadows like bruises in her perfect skin, beneath her eyes.

Though you can see that Ana would (probably) prefer not to say hello, it is not possible for you to avoid each other. You greet Ana with a friendly smile, as you would any student, ignoring her nervousness; she stammers *Hello Professor...*

Ana is embarrassed, awkward. Still, Ana manages to smile at her professor.

Telling you apologetically that she'd meant to write to you, to explain why she'd had to miss another class: there'd been a family emergency, she'd had to spend time on the phone with several relatives. Ana speaks so rapidly, in faltering English, you halfway wonder if she is telling the truth. Yet in her face, an expression of such genuine dismay, you are sure that she must be telling some part of the truth.

You are thinking *If this were a story....* You would invite Ana to have coffee with you, perhaps you would walk together in the lightly falling snow, and talk. Ana would confide in you at last, directly—as, it has seemed to you, she is confiding in you indirectly, in her writing. Ana would reveal herself the survivor of abuse, a broken and devastated household. A traumatized child in need of advice, protection...

But that does not happen. Will not happen. For this is not a story, and not a fiction. This is actual life, that does not bend easily to your fantasies.

The moment passes. You move on. You do not glance

after Ana, as, you are sure, Ana does not glance after you.

It is true, you are desperately lonely. But you understand that yours is an adult loneliness that no adolescent stranger can assuage.

*

Recalling your shock, and subsequent melancholy, when the first class of your life came to an end.

How you'd actually wept... *I will never have such wonderful students again.*

Your husband comforted you though (surely) he'd been amused.

Twenty-seven years ago.

*

As abruptly as it seemed to have begun, the semester has ended.

The final workshop in the wood-paneled seminar room at the top of the smooth-worn staircase in North Hall.

And then, reading week—between the end of classes and the start of exams. You will see students through this week, you have made appointments with each of the writers in the workshop. Following these conferences, it's likely that you will not see most of the students again.

After such intimacy, abrupt detachment. The way of teaching—semester following semester.

Professor! Hello...

There is Ana, in the doorway of your office. Accompanied by two tensely smiling adults—parents?

You don't expect this. You are totally surprised. You'd thought—what had you thought?

A lost girl, an abused girl. An orphan.

Though Ana appears to be virtually quivering with nerves, or with excitement, she has brought her parents to meet you—*Elena and Carlos Fallas.* Ana's pride in the situation, her thrilled face, shining eyes, the way she clasps her parents' hands in hers, urging them to enter your office—it is very touching, you are moved nearly to tears.

Ana's parents are so *young*. Especially the mother, who is Ana's height, small-boned, with beautiful dark eyes. Haltingly, the parents speak to you in heavily accented English. They are visiting from San Diego, they say. They have heard much about *you*.

Through a roaring in your ears, you hear Ana speaking of her favorite class, her writing class, how you helped her to write *as if your life depended upon it.*

How you'd told her—*It need not be true, your writing will make it true.*

Ana is breathless, daring. What an achievement it has been for your shyest student to have brought her parents to meet you! How long has Ana been practicing these words, this encounter...

The scene seems impossible to you. Unreal. How had you so misread Ana Fallas? Her seeming lack of interest in the seminar, and in you... her sorrowful expression, her isolation...

Had you misinterpreted, and Ana is not telling the

fullest truth now? But rather, performing for her parents? And for you?

The melancholy was not feigned, you are sure. The sorrow in her eyes. Yet—here is a very different Ana, laughing as she discreetly corrects her parents' English, vivacious and sparkling, happy.

Ana has plaited her hair into a sleekly black braid. She has painted her fingernails coral. She is wearing, not baggy clothes, but attractive bright-colored clothing that is the perfect size for her small body. The little gold cross glitters around her neck. Ana is very pretty, and she is adored by her parents. She is not an abused child, she is certainly not an orphan.

Astonishingly, you hear—*My favorite professor.*

You are determined not to betray this astonishment. You are determined to speak, despite the roaring in your ears. Assuring Ana's eager parents that Ana has been an excellent student. A very promising writer. Like few young writers, Ana can learn from criticism—constructive criticism. Ana's imagination is fertile, seemingly boundless. You are giddy as a drunkard. Words tumble from your mouth, you are shameless. You will say anything to please these people, you want only to make them happy, to make them less ill at ease in your professorial presence.

You will not confess—*I have been so mistaken about your daughter. I am ashamed....*

She is not the person I had imagined. You are not the people. Forgive me!

Ana's parents have brought you a beautifully wrapped little gift. Your heart sinks, you hope it isn't expensive.

(That size? Could be a small clock. A watch.) You have not the heart to decline their generosity, but it is considered a breach of academic ethics, at least at this university, to accept gifts from the parents of students, even small gifts.

The card from Ana you will accept, with thanks. The gift you will pass to the departmental secretary.

Ana's parents are less nervous now. They tell you how proud they are of their daughter, the first in the family to attend a four-year college. How grateful for the scholarship that brought her here—though it is so far from home. How honored to meet you.

When they leave, you stand in the doorway of your office staring after them, still disbelieving, dazed. *So mistaken. How was it possible...*

The little gift you leave on your desk for the time being. The card from Ana you open: *Thank you, Professor, for giving me the key to my life.*

*

And then, returning home later that evening.

A mild shock—the door is unlocked.

Turn the knob, and the door opens. Not for the first time since your husband has died. It is a careless habit, away for hours and the house unlocked and darkened.

You have become careless with your life. Indifferent.

Entering an empty house from which all meaning has fled.

Once, this was a *happy place*. That seems like a bad joke now.

Each room in this house is a kind of exile. You avoid most of the rooms, you keep in motion. Difficult to find a place to sit, a place where you are comfortable sitting. Almost at once, you feel restless, anxious. Your fingers clutch at the hollow in your throat, you have difficulty breathing.

He has been gone how many months. Still you cannot—quite—acknowledge the word *dead*.

Once, you'd known precisely how many weeks, days. Down to the hour.

But the house is still as deserted. This place from which happiness has drained like water seeping into earth.

You have tried to explain to your husband, as you try to explain to him so many things, for he is patient, unjudging in his new implacable silence—how you were mistaken about Ana, for so long. The stubbornness in your misperception, the hurt.

It is frightening to you, in this empty and darkened house—*What else has eluded you, that is staring you in the face? About what else have you been mistaken?*

THE MYSTERY FLOOR

–

Sloane Crosley

T*he dictionary defines an office as "a room, set of rooms, or building used as a place for commercial, professional, or bureaucratic work." I almost fell asleep on my keyboard before I finished typing that sentence, and presumably you did the same while reading it. You don't have to be a writer to redefine the traditional office, to lend a little mystery to it, to avoid phrases such as "bureaucratic work." These next two stories are proof that work does not necessitate routine. An unusual workplace often leads to the most colorful of stories.*

In Jonathan Ames's "The Depressed, the Tormented, and the Sexually Disturbed," a story is told in the form of a teleplay (a genre so seldom seen, it may be the first of its kind). A not-so-young-but-still-pretty-young man named Jonathan happens upon an unassuming office building with a plaque that reads, "Rubinstein Psychoanalytic Institute For The Depressed And Tormented." As the title of the story suggests, they also "cater to the sexually disturbed." Jonathan decides to satisfy his curiosity and soon finds himself in an office like no other. "On small side-tables, instead of magazines, there are books and pamphlets by Freud. All of the furniture seems to be from a different time." As weird as the office seems from the waiting room, it's about to get weirder. And yet the story is relatable as it removes the scrim of office decorum and opens us up to a world where doctors ask prospective patients questions like, "Do you feel capable of love?" The work done in this particular office may be unusual. The people who work here may be unusual. Jonathan himself may be unusual. But the net effect will be delightfully familiar to anyone who's worked in an eccentric place.

In case there's any doubt that a place of business is where you make it, Lee Child's "My Rules" should put that to bed. On the streets of Greenwich Village, a man with a mysterious vocation comes across two men in pinstriped suits having a debate about directions. This debate belies deeper personal and corporate conflicts. As the man tries to mediate their dispute, claiming his "field is the study of arguments, and most importantly their resolution," we discover that this is true enough—but perhaps not in the way we think. As the story progresses, we start to wonder whose office are we dealing with: the office of the two men or the roaming office of the narrator who happens upon them? Or does the office ultimately belong to the author himself, who put the "my" in "my rules?" In these unconventional workplaces, it's anyone's game.

Chapter 8

THE DEPRESSED, THE TORMENTED, AND THE SEXUALLY DISTURBED

(A SHORT STORY TOLD IN THE FORM OF A TELEPLAY)

–

Jonathan Ames

EXT. MANHATTAN BUILDING -- DAY, MID-OCTOBER

Establishing shot of an impressive Upper East Side, four-story building, made of white Italianate stone.

The building is on a cross street in the low 90s, between Madison Avenue and Fifth Avenue. It is on the south side of the street.

After the establishing shot, we ZOOM in on the building's entrance, a thick black door with a golden knob, until the camera rests - in CLOSE-UP - on a BRASS PLATE, which is next to the door and reads:

RUBINSTEIN PSYCHOANALYTIC INSTITUTE

FOR THE DEPRESSED AND THE TORMENTED.

Below that, in parentheses, are the following etched words:

(WE ALSO CATER TO THE SEXUALLY DISTURBED. BECAUSE WHO ISN'T? SEXUALLY DISTURBED THAT IS. SO DON'T BE SHY. RING THE BELL. HELP AWAITS. INSIDE. THAT'S RIGHT. RING THE BELL. YOU CAN DO IT. WE ALREADY BELIEVE IN YOU. WE DO. RING THE BELL.)

Below the brass plate is a DOOR BELL.

Just then a MAN in his late 40s (49 to be precise), crosses frame, and we follow him as he walks past the black door, heading east, away from Fifth Avenue and Central Park. He seems to glance briefly at the brass plate, but keeps going.

(During this opening scene, jaunty CLASSICAL MUSIC will be playing as score, but by the end the music will become frantic, as it often does in classical pieces - the mood of the music changing like the sky or like our own emotions.)

The man's wearing brown corduroy pants, a gray tweed blazer, and a blue Oxford shirt. He's bald, except for a close-cropped ring of fading reddish hair around the back of his head, arranged in the classic horseshoe configuration that has plagued bald men since the Roman Empire, if not before.

The camera follows the horseshoe, but then the man stops, pretends as if he just had a thought, and touches his chin.

Then he looks to his right and left, seeing if anyone notices him - no one does. He's alone for the moment on the sidewalk, a few feet past the door, and then he doubles back and quickly reads the brass plate, mouthing -

                    MAN
              (under his breath)
         The depressed and the tormented...
         the sexually disturbed...

He then looks to his right and left, checking once again if anyone has seen him, (no one has) and then, suddenly, like a cartoon character, he takes off sprinting in the direction of Fifth Avenue.

As the man runs away, his form receding, he turns left, in slapstick fashion, onto Fifth Avenue and disappears, with the camera resting on the green forest of Central Park straight ahead. From the forest, we go to BLACK.

We wait two beats. Then there's a CHYRON that reads:

TWO DAYS LATER.

Then that disappears, and we are back at the
front door to the building -

EXT. MANHATTAN BUILDING -- DAY, TWO DAYS LATER

People are walking past the door and brass
plate. The lighting is different; it's a
different time of day.

The MAN from two days earlier appears. He's
dressed in similar clothes, but he's also
wearing a cap to provide some anonymity.

The man's name is JONATHAN, though he's not
related, per se, to the author of this script,
though keep in mind that Freud said all
writing is a form of confession, or at least
I think he did.

(During this sequence, morose but then
increasingly mysterious CLASSICAL MUSIC will
be playing as score.)

Jonathan bends down to tie his shoes, even
though he's wearing loafers. He mimes the
action of shoe tying, while people cross in
front of him.

When all the people are gone and there's
a lull in the foot traffic, he hops up,
glances at the brass plate, looks to his left
and right, and then pushes the DOOR BELL.
Almost instantaneously, causing him to jump,
the door BUZZES; the lock has been released.

Jonathan fumbles with the door, but the buzzing
continues and he's able to open the door and
enter.

INT. TINY ELEVATOR -- A FEW MOMENTS LATER

Jonathan stands in a tiny, old-fashioned elevator, fretting. There's just about enough room for one person. On the wall, next to the elevator-inspection record, which is under glass, there is a photo-portrait of FREUD, also under glass.

(Gentle CLASSICAL MUSIC, like someone tip-toeing into a room, is now playing as score, or the morose and mysterious score from the previous scene could continue.)

In the corner of the ceiling of the elevator is a distorting mirror, the kind that is often, inexplicably, in the corners of the ceilings of elevators.

Jonathan looks at his DISTORTED IMAGE in the mirror and then he looks at the photo-portrait of FREUD. The elevator stops and the accordion-like door opens onto -

INT. RECEPTION AREA OF THE RUBINSTEIN PSYCHO-ANALYTIC INSTITUTE FOR THE DEPRESSED AND THE TORMENTED -- DAY, CONTINUOUS

Jonathan enters the reception area. Directly in front of him is a rather stout and powerful woman, THE RECEPTIONIST, who sits behind a large, old desk.

In the corner is a door that must lead some-where. The elevator closes behind him and the MUSICAL SCORE comes to an end.

The receptionist is in her late 60s, with an old-fashioned bosom that seems limitless and to take up most of her torso. Her well-dyed golden-brown hair is in an unusual vertical bun above her head, twisting upward like a challah.

In this reception area, in addition to the receptionist, there are three chairs for patients to sit on while waiting.

On small side tables, instead of magazines, there are books and pamphlets by Freud. All the furniture seems to be from a different time. It's of the past.

> RECEPTIONIST
> (cheerful)
> Hello there! Come in, young man.

Jonathan is middle-aged and bald, with hysterical digestion, but he *does* feel like a young man.

His life has whipped past him so quickly and with so much confusion that, even though he's approaching the age of 50, he feels emotionally like some mixture of a 26 year-old and a seven-year-old, perhaps adding up to the mean age of 33.

Which is, ostensibly, an important age, since that was the age Jesus had achieved at the time of his death, though having Jonathan be 33 was not intentional on this author's part, especially since Jonathan is actually 49 in this story, while the writer himself is 53.

All this to say that, when the receptionist called Jonathan "young man," it felt perfectly natural to him.

But, anxious at being at the Rubinstein Psychoanalytic Institute, he's frozen in place in front of the elevator.

The receptionist, naturally, notices this bit
of catatonia and says, sweetly -

                    RECEPTIONIST (CONT'D)
          Come in. Come in, dear boy. Tell me
          why you're here.

Responsive to the commands of others and
naturally obedient, Jonathan takes three
steps, and he's in front of the desk. He
removes his cap like Oliver Twist and stammers -

                    JONATHAN
          Well, you see...I...I...was on the
          street and...I...was intrigued and
          well...I...you see...have always...
          been in a lot of pain...but...
          well...I...

                    RECEPTIONIST
          You're interested in analysis. Is
          that it?

                    JONATHAN
          Yes.

                    RECEPTIONIST
          And you feel stuck in life and inca-
          pable of change?

                    JONATHAN
                (beat, looks down, then
                up with bashful eyes)
          Yes. Very much so.

                    RECEPTIONIST
          And you repeat destructive patterns
          of behavior and destructive patterns
          of thinking and don't feel like a real

human being much of the time?

                    JONATHAN
Yes. All of that.

                    RECEPTIONIST
Good. Have a seat. My husband, Dr.
Schwartz-Gelson, will evaluate you
in a few minutes.

                    JONATHAN
Schwartz-Gelson?

                    RECEPTIONIST
Yes. I'm Schwartz, he's Gelson.

                    JONATHAN
I see....

                    RECEPTIONIST
Well, have a seat, he's been waiting
for you.

                    JONATHAN
But...but I just got here.

                    RECEPTIONIST
He's always waiting for the next pa-
tient, and you're the next patient.
Have a seat.

She smiles, gestures to the chairs, and he
starts to head over. She presses a button on
an intercom box, says into it:

                    RECEPTIONIST (CONT'D)
Jonathan is here.

Jonathan turns at his name, smiles, sits down,
and just as he sits, the DOOR in the corner
flies open and a very short, old black man

emerges, wearing a tweed three-piece suit and tie. This is DOCTOR SCHWARTZ-GELSON, and he bellows:

DR. SCHWARTZ-GELSON
Jonathan, so good to see you!

Jonathan, shocked at the bellowing, though having just sat, jettisons to his feet, clutching his hat.

(The rhythm of this should all be quite rapid - receptionist speaks into the intercom, Jonathan sits, the door flies open, the doctor bellows, and Jonathan bolts upward.)

Dr. Schwartz-Gelson is about five-foot-two, compact like an artillery shell, and quite bald, except for a grizzled horseshoe of silver around his luminous dark-brown skull.

He strides over in Jonathan's direction, but stops to go behind the receptionist's desk, where he gives the receptionist, his wife, quite the kiss, tilting her head back.

Sitting, she's as tall as he is, and her challah-bun is even taller, and the camera pans down from the kiss to a close-up of a PICTURE on the receptionist's desk.

It shows Dr. and Mrs. Schwartz-Gelson at a black-tie psychonanalytic function: his arm is around her waist, his head is level with her prodigious bosom, and they smile brightly for the camera.

Then we cut to Jonathan, confused, watching them kiss. And then, finally, the kiss is over - the receptionist is flushed and stimulated - and Dr. Schwartz-Gelson heads over to Jonathan, offering his hand.

>   DR. SCHWARTZ-GELSON (CONT'D)
>   I'm Dr. Schwartz-Gelson. I'm so glad
>   you came in today, Jonathan.

Jonathan timidly offers his hand in return, while towering over Schwartz-Gelson. Jonathan is six feet tall and looks like a giant next to the diminutive analyst.

(But inside, Jonathan feels shorter than the doctor, as if he were looking up at him, which is not uncommon for Jonathan. He usually thinks that he's smaller than most people. In fact, when he sees pictures of himself next to others, even tiny women, he's surprised to observe that he's in fact larger.

All this can be explained, perhaps, by his feeling that a part of himself is stuck at the age of seven, a kind of body and age dysmorphia rolled into one.

But why the age of seven? Perhaps a trauma froze him there, like the two lovers in Pompeii, forever wrapped in each other's arms. Except Jonathan was alone.)

The doctor shakes Jonathan's hand, enthusiastically, and then says:

>   DR. SCHWARTZ-GELSON (CONT'D)
>   Come with me, lad.

They leave the reception area and go through the open door, which leads to a very large office area.

INT. ANALYTIC OFFICE SPACE -- DAY, CONTINUOUS

After they enter, the doctor closes the door behind them.

This office space, which is the size and length of a basketball court, has a central, wide carpeted passageway.

To the right and to the left of this passageway, there are six offices, enclosed in glass with glass doors, adding up to a total of twelve offices.

And while the reception area felt like it was out of the past, this office space is quite modernistic, yet warm.

At the end of the passageway, like at the top of the letter T, there are three spaces, from left to right: a kitchen-lounge with a fridge, coffee-maker, and cafe tables; a large office, behind clear glass, like all the other offices; and then a large office behind frosted glass.

Dr. Schwartz-Gelson leads Jonathan down the passageway, and Jonathan steals little glimpses into the offices on his right and left. Behind each large window, an ANALYSAND lies on a narrow analytic couch, and sitting in a chair, slightly behind the analysand, taking notes, is their ANALYST.

(In psychoanalysis, analyst and patient don't look at each other to help encourage the patient to free-associate and not worry about performing for the doctor.)

Though everyone is quite exposed in their glass boxes at the Rubinstein Institute, one gets a sense of privacy, nevertheless, as if the patients and doctors were in their own worlds with each other: one talking, one listening.

Jonathan and Dr. Schwartz-Gelson reach the end of the passageway.

          DR. SCHWARTZ-GELSON
       (gestures to the lounge,
       which is to the left)
This is the lounge where patients can mingle, if they like. We always have a fresh pot of coffee going.

          JONATHAN
Do the doctors mingle?

          DR. SCHWARTZ-GELSON
Never with the patients. An analyst has to maintain a certain remove, you know.

Jonathan nods as if he understands. Then Dr. Schwartz-Gelson points to the office directly in front of them, and behind the large glass window we see two BUNK BEDS, made from a total of four analytic couches. In between the two bunk beds and slightly behind them is an ELEVATED CHAIR, like a lifeguard's chair.

          DR. SCHWARTZ-GELSON (CONT'D)
       (gesturing to this room)
This is where I conduct overnight group analysis.

          JONATHAN
I didn't know that there was such a thing as overnight group analysis.

          DR. SCHWARTZ-GELSON
It's not common. I....well, I invented it. It's very helpful for dream-work.

He smiles shyly, and then gripping Jonathan's elbow says -

> DR. SCHWARTZ-GELSON (CONT'D)
> And this is my office -

He leads Jonathan to the last office at the end of the large room, on the far right, the one behind frosted glass. They enter the office -

INT. DR. SCHWARTZ-GELSON'S OFFICE -- CONTINUOUS

This office has wall-to-wall bookshelves, with a thousand or more volumes. The room feels like a private library, and furnishing-wise seems to be out of the past, like the reception area.

It has two leather chairs and an analytic couch. There's also a desk, where Dr. Schwartz-Gelson works on his articles for psychonanalytic journals. His emphasis for many years has been the importance of compassion, breast-feeding, and toilet training.

> DR. SCHWARTZ-GELSON
> (gesturing to the leather
> chair, which is not next
> to the couch)
> Have a seat, Jonathan.

Jonathan sits. Dr. Schwartz-Gelson takes a steno pad and pen from his desk and sits on the leather chair, which is next to the couch. They are across from each other.

> JONATHAN
> I don't get to lie on the couch?

DR. SCHWARTZ-GELSON
Not yet. In this interview, I'm
evaluating whether or not you are
actually a candidate for analysis.
Not everyone is.

JONATHAN
I see.

DR. SCHWARTZ-GELSON
But before we begin, do you have any
questions?

JONATHAN
Yes. How much will this cost?

DR. SCHWARTZ-GELSON
Nothing! This is a free clinic. Has
been for 47 years!

JONATHAN
I didn't know that.

DR. SCHWARTZ-GELSON
Didn't you read about us on the
Internet?

JONATHAN
No. I was drawn in by the brass plate
down below.

DR. SCHWARTZ-GELSON
Oh, good, I wrote that myself. Well,
what you would've learned on our web-
page is that the Rubinstein Foundation, which made its fortune in
liquor stores and parking lots, gave
us a massive endowment in the late
'60s. Adolph Rubinstein, the family
patriarch, credited psychoanalysis

with helping with his stockmarket
decisions, as well as curing his 30-
year struggle with premature ejacu-
lation, back pain, and diarrhea, and
so he generously wanted to give to
others what had been given to him.

          JONATHAN
That's incredible. Well, if I do
this, if you think I'm a candidate,
how often will I have to come here?

          DR. SCHWARTZ-GELSON
Four times a week for 50-minute
sessions. And the average analysis
lasts about five years, but many go
longer. So you're looking at some
where between a thousand and two
thousand sessions.

Jonathan closes his eyes and puts his hands
over his face: *Even though it's free, what a
commitment!*

Dr. Schwartz-Gelson responds to this non-
verbal gesture -

          DR. SCHWARTZ-GELSON (CONT'D)
It takes time, Jonathan, to effect
change. Human beings are very stub-
born. Would you like to be able to
change?

Jonathan takes his hands away from his face,
opens his eyes.

          JONATHAN
Yes. I want to change. I want to
grow up before my life is over.

DR. SCHWARTZ-GELSON
Excellent. Let's get started then.

The doctor readies his pen and steno-pad.

DR. SCHWARTZ-GELSON (CONT'D)
I'm just going to ask a few painless
questions.

JONATHAN
OK -

DR. SCHWARTZ-GELSON
How long were you breast-fed?

JONATHAN
(immediately upset)
I thought you said the questions
would be painless!

DR. SCHWARTZ-GELSON
(firm)
Answer the question!

JONATHAN
Only two weeks and I'm still upset
about it!

DR. SCHWARTZ-GELSON
So you're a breast man? Been quest-
ing for the nipple ever since?

JONATHAN
(in a whisper)
Yes.

Jonathan smiles weakly, a bit ashamed.

              DR. SCHWARTZ-GELSON
Don't be embarrassed. I'm also a
breast man. You may have guessed as
much when you met my wife, Ruth.

              JONATHAN
Ruth?

              DR. SCHWARTZ-GELSON
Mrs. Schwartz-Gelson.

              JONATHAN
Oh, yes, of course. Right, sorry.

              DR. SCHWARTZ-GELSON
Are you married?

              JONATHAN
No.

              DR. SCHWARTZ-GELSON
Are you single?

              JONATHAN
Yes.

              DR. SCHWARTZ-GELSON
Would you like a companion?

              JONATHAN
Yes.

              DR. SCHWARTZ-GELSON
Do you feel capable of love?

              JONATHAN
I'm...I'm not sure.

>   DR. SCHWARTZ-GELSON
> Do you like to eat in or go out?

>   JONATHAN
> Go out.

>   DR. SCHWARTZ-GELSON
> Right.

He looks down at his pad and writes what we
hear him muttering to himself, which is the
first time he has scribbled something, and we
can see on the PAD what he writes down:

>   DR. SCHWARTZ-GELSON (CONT'D)
>   (writing, muttering)
> *Likes to go out.*
>   (then he looks up from
>   his pad and says -)
> And how often do you think of sui-
> cide?

>   JONATHAN
> What?
>   (beat, then in a whisper,
>   lowering his head)
> Often.

>   DR. SCHWARTZ-GELSON
> Are you going to hurt yourself to-
> day? After you leave here?

>   JONATHAN
>   (looks up, vulnerable)
> No.

>   DR. SCHWARTZ-GELSON
> Are you sure?

JONATHAN

Yes. It's always just in my mind. I could never actually do it. I would never want to hurt my mother that way. She's 80.

DR. SCHWARTZ-GELSON

Promise you won't hurt yourself?

JONATHAN

I promise.

DR. SCHWARTZ-GELSON

I can trust you on this?

JONATHAN

Yes. You can trust me.

DR. SCHWARTZ-GELSON

Good. I believe you. Do you have a dog?

JONATHAN

Yes.

DR. SCHWARTZ-GELSON

What's the dog's name?

JONATHAN

Louis.

Dr. Schwartz-Gelson then slams the steno pad shut, with a big smile on his face, as if hearing the name "Louis" cinched the deal.

DR. SCHWARTZ-GELSON

Well, that's it! You're a prime candidate for analysis. Congratulations!

>   JONATHAN
>   (excited)
> Really?

>   DR. SCHWARTZ-GELSON
> Yes! You are about to begin an in-
> credible adventure. Freud called it
> the talking cure for a reason: You
> will talk yourself into wellness,
> tapping into your own innate wisdom,
> and you'll have the chance to know
> the one person who has been such a
> mystery to you all along - *yourself*!

He then strides over to Jonathan, offering his
hand. Jonathan stands and they shake, and
while they shake, the doctor says -

>   DR. SCHWARTZ-GELSON (CONT'D)
> I think you would be best served by
> having a woman analyst, for reasons
> of transference. And in my opinion
> Chiara is the one for you.

>   JONATHAN
> Chiara?

They stop shaking hands.

>   DR. SCHWARTZ-GELSON
> Yes. She's from Trieste but speaks
> English beautifully. James Joyce
> lived in Trieste, if that's of any
> interest to you.
>   (he then looks at his
>   watch)
> She'll be available in ten minutes.
> In the meantime, you can wait in the
> lounge and have a cup of coffee.

He leads Jonathan to the door, and as Jonathan exits, he smacks Jonathan in the ass. Jonathan, now out in the main room, turns and has a shocked look on his face.

> DR. SCHWARTZ-GELSON (CONT'D)
> Was that inappropriate?

> JONATHAN
> Yes!

> DR. SCHWARTZ-GELSON
> (genuine)
> Sorry!

Dr. Schwartz-Gelson then slams his office door shut. We close on Jonathan's bewildered face.

INT. KITCHEN-LOUNGE -- A FEW MINUTES LATER

Jonathan sits at one of the cafe tables, sipping a coffee. Then a bell rings, like a school bell, and analysands pour out of the offices. Some leave, and several head for the lounge. They are an interesting mix of race, age, and gender.

There's a murmur of talking. Jonathan tries not to make eye contact with anyone, but hears a snippet of conversation between two analysands by the coffee maker -

> ANALYSAND #1/A MAN
> (pouring a cup of coffee)
> ...We worked on a dream I had where
> the bottoms of my feet were slit
> open, like envelopes, and balls of
> pus, like marbles, rolled out.

                    ANALYSAND #2/A WOMAN
                      (not impressed)
            Oh, I've had that dream -

As Jonathan listens to this, a beautiful
WOMAN in an elegant work dress approaches him.
But he doesn't see her since he's trying to
secretly spy on the analysands.

This is CHIARA. She's in her early 40s and
looks like Sophia Loren. She interrupts
Jonathan's surreptitious eavesdropping.

                       CHIARA
                (a slight Italian accent)
            Are you Jonathan?

Jonathan turns, startled. From his POV, we go
close on Chiara's face. She seems to be in a
halo of light.

                      JONATHAN
            Yes. I'm Jonathan.

                       CHIARA
            I'm Chiara. I'm ready for you.

She reaches down and offers her hand. He takes
her hand and rises out of his chair. She then
leads him, like a child, to her office.

Chapter 9

MY RULES

–

Lee Child

As planned I visited three bars near Washington Square, and as expected I came away satisfied. After that I walked west into the quiet afternoon, and on the stroke of three o'clock I turned into Barrow Street, which was silent and deserted. No one was up yet. Too early. No doubt times have changed since then. Now I'm sure they buy apartments for a million dollars. Maybe two million dollars. Now I'm sure they work all day to pay the note. But way back long ago in the times I'm talking about, the residents of Barrow Street didn't do much of anything at all. Certainly never before eight or ten in the evening. Hence currently silent and deserted. Slumber was continuing. I was all alone. There was no sound. I could have been in Kansas.

Until two guys walked in the other way. Lost, I assumed. No other reason for them to be there. Not in that historical era. They were dressed in pinstripe suits, dark blue, with snowy starched shirts and silk neckties cinched tight. One guy was maybe 50, and the other was maybe 30. Maybe a partner and an associate. Or a bank president and a favored VP. That kind of dynamic. The older guy had pale eyebrows and colorless blond hair going gray. Right there and then I bet on the weekends he wore pink pants and went to the Hamptons. That kind of guy. Probably had a sailboat. The 30-year-old was shorter and squatter and had a head of oiled black hair. On a bathroom scale he would have outweighed his boss by 20 pounds or more, but the older guy was in charge. That was clear. He was a beaky, patrician kind of a character. Authority was coming off him in waves.

I figured they had come north from Wall Street to get a private lunch away from prying eyes. Probably because they had important matters to discuss. I figured the older guy's wife had picked out the restaurant. Word of mouth from a neighbor, or a mention in a hip magazine. Probably the two guys had been unimpressed. Now they had forgotten where their car was parked. Hence their random turn into silent and deserted Barrow Street. No other reason. Nothing for them there. Or for me, or for anyone.

Or maybe there was.

They were arguing. I saw it clearly when they got close. The older guy was moving as awkward as a stilt walker, and the younger guy was all seized up with frustration. He was stumping along, as rigid as a mannequin. I heard him hiss something about a grandfather, and I heard the older guy hiss something back, and for a second I wondered if they were related. Father and son, maybe, arguing over a legacy. But ultimately I thought not. They were too close in age, and too far apart in appearance.

"Gentlemen," I said. "May I help you with something?"

The older guy seemed to find nothing weird about the question. A guy like that got asked greasy questions all the time. He lived in a world of doormen and bellhops and maître d's and valet parkers and secretaries and assistants' assistants. Perhaps he thought the Village employed concierges, standing ready to render services if required to people just like him. My appearance helped the illusion. As always I was dressed in a dull suit, unremarkable and anonymous. It was neat, but a little worn and faded. A little shiny at the knees and elbows. Just like a person would wear, who worked a hotel lobby five days a week.

The older guy looked at me but said nothing at first. He was trying to hide how mad he was. That kind of old-fashioned character never washed his linens in public. Wasn't raised that way. Then he saw how he might score a subtle point.

He said, "We're looking for the garage on Sullivan Street. My colleague insists it's in this direction."

I knew the place he meant. It had a big sign and a guy with an orange flag. He was supposed to wave people in. In reality most of the time he sat in the sunshine in a folding chair, and now and then twitched his flag like a cow flicking flies with its tail.

Sullivan Street was in the opposite direction entirely.

"Let me guess," I said. "You ate at that new French place."

"As a matter of fact we did," the older guy said, politely enough, in a measured cadence, but through tight lips and ground teeth. He was still angry.

"Did you like it?" I asked.

"Not much," the younger guy said. "They served us pigs' cheeks."

Which I guessed was a subtle score of his own, if in fact his boss's wife had indeed recommended the place. Which I was sure she had. They wouldn't have relied on a secretary or an assistant's assistant. Not if they wanted to be off the record and away from prying eyes.

I said, "I'm afraid Sullivan Street is not in this direction."

The younger guy looked down at the sidewalk. His opening bid about the pigs' cheeks had been countered by his own geographical error. He was back level. Like 30-all in tennis. Disappointing. But his own fault.

"You must have gotten turned around," I said. "Maybe you were preoccupied."

He didn't answer.

His boss said to me, "Just tell us how to get to Sullivan Street."

"That was my intention," I said. "Now I'm not sure I should."

"Why on earth wouldn't you?"

"I might be wasting my breath," I said. "Turning the right way out of a restaurant door ain't exactly rocket science. Especially when you just walked the route a couple hours before. Yet you got turned around. I'm afraid it might happen again. Clearly you have things on your mind that are interfering with the retention of unfamiliar but fundamentally simple information. As a result, I worry I could go to all kinds of trouble explaining the turns, but you might be lost again after a block and a half. Not good for you, not good for me."

They both stared at me.

"I'm from the university," I said, without mentioning which one, because I didn't really know any. Students are no good to me. I said, "My field is the study of the psychology of arguments, and most importantly their resolution. But I apologize. This is none of my business. Although seriously, I feel obliged to point out you won't remember the turns until you end the dispute."

The older guy said, "How can you know that?"

"I wrote the book, literally. No one knows more than me about arguments, and what they do to people, and how to fix them."

The guy took another look at my suit. Skeptical at first, then less. I could have been a professor. Maybe eminent, but badly paid and a little eccentric.

He said, "How do you fix them?"

"First we admit out loud exactly what they are. We don't try to pretty them up. We acknowledge up front that they're contests. They're adversarial, antagonistic, and gladiatorial. They're the intellectual equivalents of fights to the death. Stand shoulder to shoulder, but a yard apart."

"What?"

"Shoulder to shoulder, but a yard apart," I said again.

These were guys who no doubt considered themselves sturdily contemptuous of bullshit, but nevertheless they shuffled into line, a yard apart, staring dead ahead. The older guy did it more naturally. Prep school, I thought. They were always lining up for something.

"Good," I said.

I looped around behind them and stepped into the yard gap between them, facing the same way, looking straight ahead. Like we were three actors about to take a bow at the end of a play. I put my hands on their wrists. I raised the older guy's hand up high.

"On my right," I said. "The undisputed heavyweight champion of the world."

I lowered his hand again. I raised up the younger guy's.

"On my left," I said. "The challenger."

Then I let go of their wrists and stepped forward and turned around to face them. The three of us made a tight triangle shape on the silent sidewalk.

"Now we know where we are," I said. "Now we wait for the bell to ring, and then we start trading punches. Except we don't, because we're civilized people. We do it with words instead. So go ahead. I'm the referee. The challenger should take the first swing. Generally the challenger always does."

The younger guy said, "Well, I, I, it's an office matter, I don't know, I mean I'm not sure how I could—"

"Short and sharp," I said. "Make your case. Tell the story. Make your points. Like punches. Fast hands. Nothing long."

He said, "I was asked to take a hundred thousand out of the maintenance budget."

I nodded, and held my hand up, palm out like a stop sign, and I looked at the older guy.

"Accurate?" I asked him.

He nodded.

He said, "It's a company-wide economy drive. Every department has to contribute. Common sense, really. I have to be realistic."

"Are you the boss?"

"Chairman, CEO, majority stockholder, and grandson of the founder."

I turned back to the younger guy.

I said, "And you are?"

He said, "Vice president in charge of delivering whatever the chairman wants."

"Are you succeeding?"

"More than," he said, a little bitterly. "I got an idea and worked out how we could cut nightly cleaning in half, and repaint every eight years instead of three. Which overall would save us much more than a hundred thousand a year. Perhaps fifty percent more. It's a gift. It's free money. It's insane not to take it."

I nodded again, and held up my hand again, and looked at the older guy.

"Accurate?" I asked him.

He started sputtering and smacking his lips and huffing and puffing and waving his arms around, like he was casting about for the perfect devastating response. Like he wanted it to be a paragraph long, with a beginning, and a middle, and an end.

"Short and sharp," I said.

"It's impractical," he said.

"Was your colleague's statement accurate? About the financial savings?"

"Technically, I suppose."

"But impractical."

"Worse than that," he said. "It's completely ridiculous. And a waste of my time. I need real-world solutions, not pie-in-the-sky fantasies."

I turned back to the VP in charge of delivering.

I said, "I assume you object to that description."

"Yes, I do," he said. "In fact it's a totally real-world solution. It's a huge saving, and a huge win-win too, because we can spin it in a totally positive way."

"What's the idea?"

"Ban smoking in the workplace."

"Smoking what?"

"Cigarettes."

"You mean a person couldn't smoke a cigarette at his desk while he's doing his work?"

"That's my idea."

I looked at the older guy.

"See?" he said. "It's a stupid fantasy."

The younger guy was getting all worked up. He said, "Half of what we spend on nightly cleaning is related either directly or indirectly to smoking. Ashtrays need to be emptied and cleaned, obviously, but significant dusting and vacuuming time is at stake too. I commissioned a study. We could cut the crews in half. We could get them out of the building before their night rates kick in. But the real money is in not having to paint the place every five minutes. We could go at least eight years. Maybe ten, if we wanted. The reduced disruption alone would save us a fortune. There are all kinds of financial benefits. Fire insurance would go down. And on top of everything else, we can sell it as a health thing. Don't you see? It's perfect. We can claim all we want is for folks to be healthy. There's no answer to that."

I asked, "Why did you mention a grandfather?"

"We didn't," the older guy said. "I insisted we should at least grandfather in the rights of people already with us."

"Which is totally ridiculous," the younger guy said. "It totally defeats the point. We would make no savings at all."

He was so agitated he took an involuntary step forward.

No meant threat, I'm sure, but the older guy twitched with some kind of an ancient reflex and took a step up of his own. They went nose to nose.

The younger guy said, "You asked me to find a hundred thousand dollars."

The older guy said, "Find them somewhere else."

"Why pass this up?"

"It's absurd."

"It's by far the best option."

"My workplace," the older guy said. "My rules."

The younger guy pressed closer still. I put my hands back to back and pushed them apart with my palms. I patted the younger guy on the chest. Right on his tie. Rhythmically and reassuringly. I saw a guy calm a horse that way, on a TV show. The guy felt like a horse. There was heat coming off him. The older guy stepped back, so my other hand fell away naturally. At that point I stopped patting. We all shuffled back to our triangle shape, a little wider than before.

"Good," I said. "Now we know where we are."

"Do we?" the older guy asked.

"Your colleague had an excellent idea, except unfortunately it was too far ahead of its time to be of any use in terms of your present-day fiscal predicament. Therefore you're giving him your blessing to pursue a second-best alternative, which you acknowledge will be vastly inferior in every possible way, but hey, needs must. While simultaneously keeping his excellent idea up your sleeve and promising to unleash it the very next day after someone else does it first. While hoping your colleague will still be around on that distant date, to take all the credit. I'm sure he'll be president of something by then. He's a far-seeing man."

They both straightened up a little, out of their defensive crouches, and they clicked their necks and rolled their shoulders, visibly relaxing, like mighty forces disassembling vast and dangerous arsenals.

I said, "Go back the way you came, turn left on Bleecker, and Sullivan is the sixth cross street you'll see. Turn left for the garage."

They nodded, kind of cautiously, maybe embarrassed or a little sheepish, and they walked away, back the way they had come, and they turned left on Bleecker, out of my sight. I walked the other way, with their watches and their wallets, and a diamond tie pin, and a silver-plated cigarette lighter, and a pair of rose gold cuff links. Which, added to the pockets I had picked in the bars near Washington Square, made for a damn good day.

I had a smile on my face.

The streets of Greenwich Village, baby.

My workplace. My rules.

THE SOUND OF THE
VACUUM CLEANER

Sloane Crosley

*A*nd then, one day, just like that, it's over. Whatever relationship you currently have with office life, it will change. Maybe you retire. Maybe you transfer to a different city. Maybe you get fired. Time passes and you step off one career carousel onto another and another and another. Only after the carousel stops can you see how differently it looks from when you first stepped on.

When Alain Mabanckou's "The Miraculous Hand" begins, the narrator is the Director of Human Resources for a large company in Paris. He fetishizes the trappings of his office, stocking his refrigerator with Perrier and beer, and his bookshelves with great works of literature that reflect and assert his wide array of cultural interests. He has two secretaries perched outside his "150 square meters of space designated exclusively for me." But when high-placed government emissaries from his native Congo convince him to uproot his carefully curated life, things go pear-shaped. First, there's the horror of an open floor plan. Second, the horror that some people might actually prefer it. He finds *it difficult to let go of the familiar hallmarks of success, of a corporate ladder fully climbed. Home is not as he left it, and neither is work.*

Finally, there is Billy Collins's "My Father's Office," a tribute to workplaces past. In sharp detail, he immortalizes "the miracle of triplicate" and tear-off calendars with "the days disappearing one page at a time." The poem has an enchantingly melancholy feel, a grown-up's Goodnight Moon *waving goodbye to paperweights, hat racks, and rotary phones. The poem speaks directly to anyone who's ever strolled down a stretch of gum-flecked city pavement and frozen at the sight of the building in which she spent, say, nine years of her professional life before quitting to become a full-time writer. She watches the revolving doors, seeing through glass to an elevator inside, searching for the past in the form of old faces and familiar conversations.*

Ah, the flash of betrayal to see how it's all gone on without her! Other workers have sprung up from the ashes of her paperwork. And yet she can't help but smile. This may no longer be the place that raised her, that taught her everything she knew, that paid to keep the lights on in her first apartment. But this is that place for some

one else, someone else whose life will be shaped
by where she works, just as this narrator's life
is being shaped in this apartment right now,
typing in these pajamas, sitting in this living
room I have come to know only as my office.

Chapter 10

THE MIRACULOUS HAND
–
Alain Mabanckou

When I still held the position of Director of Human Resources in Paris, I had a large private office on the tenth floor in a modern building in the 7th arrondissement, near the Champ-de-Mars. The office had a view of the Eiffel Tower, and I was proud to stand in front of the huge, glazed window watching tourists from all over the world visit this historical monument built in 1889 by Gustave Eiffel at the time France was celebrating the 100th anniversary of its revolution.

What other Parisian office was better located than mine? I had to live up to this privilege. I always dressed in a suit and tie, with polished shoes and trimmed hair. I carried a black leather briefcase weighed down by files that I had already started working on during the morning commute. My driver would hasten to open the door and say, "Have a good day, Monsieur Director," as soon as I got out. The moment I entered the lobby I was greeted with further deference, and I nodded my head slightly and offered a faint smile. Then I pressed the elevator button, which led me up to the tenth floor. I walked down a huge hallway, greeting my colleagues and stopping for a few minutes at reception to view the list of my appointments before entering my office to speak with my secretaries, two French women whom I had recruited as soon as they had completed their master's in public relations. I had chosen them, in large part, because they, too, had made it through the University of Paris-Dauphine, in the 16th arrondissement, where I was a student 20 years earlier.

I was one of the most respected people in my field. People were intimidated as soon as they crossed the threshold of my office, perhaps because of the red carpet that covered the 150 square meters of space designated exclusively for me. The walls were painted sky blue, which had a relaxing effect (no small feat) on the seriousness of my line of work: hiring the right people for the right position, but also announcing to fathers or mothers that they will no longer be a part of the company and that a termination procedure has been initiated against them. No matter what, a Director of Human Resources will always be blamed. He will be criticized, on the one hand, for not having hired the best candidate in the first place, and on the other because he has fired some poor soul with children to feed, funeral costs, a mortgage to repay, and whatever else.

Yes, the Director of Human Resources is a cold monster, a killer without remorse, a chainsaw with sharp teeth, a man or a woman whose job is to take all the blame. It is for this reason that he must have a sizable office, so that whoever enters for a job interview or for notification of a termination procedure does not feel cornered, as if caught in a trap.

It is easy for a Director to announce good news like, "Your candidacy has caught our attention, and we will be offering you a position." But it is painful when he has to say something along the lines of, "As stated in our previous meeting, held on March 12, we have decided to proceed with your dismissal."

I did this type of work for over 20 years, and I was still doing it in Paris until last month.

But now I've left France and accepted an offer from the National Electricity Company of the Congo in Pointe-Noire. If they came to recruit me in Paris, it was because word of my good reputation had reached my homeland, and they knew, as I was told, that I was one of the few Africans who hired and fired white people in Europe. It was ridiculous for my countrymen to see my professional success as a racial victory. In my work, I don't care if people are black, white, or rainbow-colored. I studied labor law to become as competent as possible in all aspects of the job, regardless of a candidate's racial or social status, and started my career at a very young age. After placing at the top of my class in graduate studies at the University of Paris-Dauphine, I immediately began working in the Department of Human Resources for the Suez Group, France's leading water and waste-management company. Very quickly, because of my ability to adapt to and motivate my colleagues, I climbed the professional ladder, first as assistant to the Director and then, when he was poached by the competition, as his successor.

After two decades at the Suez Group, I felt like I belonged to a real family. I was satisfied, especially with my office, for which I had requested an expansion whose renovation would be according to my own design. I arranged a round wooden table in the middle of the room for meetings with my team. The walls were decorated with paintings that I had bought all over the world during my professional travels. A fully stocked refrigerator allowed my guests to feel comfortable when I offered them a fresh beer or Perrier. The large sofa, placed just the right distance from the fridge, was one of the things I liked the most, and I'd unwind there before afternoon appointments. At around two p.m., I'd prepare a coffee with cream in the lovely Nespresso machine that my colleagues gave me on my fifteenth anniversary with the company. On a long wooden sideboard, I had placed African statuettes, many from Central Africa. On this table, there were also shells and my collection of exotic insects from Madagascar and the Comoros. I preferred to work either on the sofa or at the round table where I had the best view of the Eiffel Tower and planes crossing the Paris sky. It's also important to emphasize that in my office library were not only books on my profession, but also the great literary classics: Charles Dickens, John Steinbeck, Ernest Hemingway, Chinua Achebe, Alexandre Dumas, Camara Laye, Fernando Pessoa, and even Gabriel García Márquez, Dostoyevsky, and Dino Buzzati. All these illustrious writers accompanied me in silence, watched me working, having meetings, chatting with colleagues who themselves were very impressed that I was drawn to books beyond the subjects connected to my work.

To access the office, you had to first make an appointment, then pass through the lair of my two secretaries, who liked to keep people waiting in a room just across the way that had a mounted television showing promotional films of our company.

Yes, I could have been content with this extraordinary professional success. But last year, Congo's Finance Minister came to see me without scheduling an appointment. I agreed to receive him and his advisors because it's not every day that a minister shows up. He paced around my office, admiring my works of art and flipping through a few books in my library. Then he got to the heart of the matter:

"You are likely wondering, my dear René Massengo, the reason for my visit...."

"Minister, I will not presume to ask, but you will understand that I am surprised to receive such an honor...."

"Well, I will get straight to the point...."

He took a breath and continued: "Your place is not here in Paris, Monsieur Massengo.... We need your expertise back home. Your experience will be very useful in the development of our National Electricity Company...."

The Minister expressed regret that most African executives no longer return home but rather remain in Europe or migrate to the United States. Before leaving, he handed me his business card and said, while warmly shaking my hand: "Think about my proposal carefully, dear René Massengo, and call me if you really love your country and you are tired of working for another nation."

I phoned my parents in the Congo. My father and mother were thrilled at the idea that I might come back to Pointe-Noire. My younger sister had a different opinion.

"What will you do in the Congo? You'd be crazy to give up everything in France where you're even in charge of white people! Don't come back here, please!"

But I could not stop thinking about the minister's proposal. I could not sleep. I phoned him, and after talking for half an hour I gave him a definitive answer. I would resign from the Suez Group to go to work at the National Electricity Company of the Congo.

The Suez Group, for its part, tried to keep me, but I was more and more enthusiastic about being of service to my countrymen.

Two months later, I was free to go. I left everything behind, which was not very complicated since I was still single, without children, without a girlfriend at the age of 45. But this is the path I have chosen, and it would take too long to explain it all here....

I arrived in the Congo a week before some terrible news. I heard on Congolese National Radio that the Finance Minister had died of a heart attack. The position remained vacant for more than a month while I was in the country without work. I was staying at a hotel in Brazzaville, waiting for the official decree of my new position to be signed by the new Minister, whom I did not know and who was a 70-year-old man whose haughty disposition annoyed me every time we spoke on the phone. He spoke to me as if I were a bother to him and would schedule me for appointments only to cancel at the last minute. During that time, I personally paid for the cost of my hotel, including the expenses for my parents' and sister's multiple trips from Pointe-Noire to visit me.

When the contract was finally signed—without my ever meeting the new Minister face-to-face—I booked a Sunday afternoon flight and landed in Pointe-Noire one hour later. A very modest accommodation awaited me downtown. The residence was situated on the third floor. The view was of the Adolphe Cissé Hospital morgue, where I saw families in tears and corpses carried on stretchers like animals....

I then visited my new place of work to meet the people who would become my colleagues and above all to settle into the office that had been assigned to me as the new Director of Human Resources for the National Electricity Company of the Congo.

When I encountered the executive offices, I almost fainted. The former minister had promised that I would be so delighted with my office that I would spend more time at work than at home.

At first, surveying this place that everyone called *open space*, I told myself that it must be meant for my team and that my own office was located somewhere else. But the Logistics Manager told me that I, too, would be working there, among the other employees, because the new Minister wanted to reduce inequalities between executives and other employees. This Minister, who had studied in the United States, wanted to ensure, as in some offices there, that everyone could speak openly and work together without division. It was a new way of operating that seemed to have been increasingly successful in state-run Congolese companies.

For me, who'd only ever had the experience of working in a private office, I considered this space nothing more than a glorified shed, a depot where people came and went, spoke loudly, burst out laughing at any moment without focus on their work. Tables were glued together, files were in messy piles here and there next to old computers whose screens were affixed with Post-Its identifying the names of their users. How would my so-called collaborators be able to work comfortably if they felt that I was always watching them?

These offices were brand new. A few months later, I learned that at one time the premises of the National Electricity Company were located in a large tower near the Victory Palace Hotel. The new minister had placed several of his advisors there, each of whom had his own office, and no one was working in an *open space....*

Something made me really angry one morning, and I brought the whole team together and suggested that we write a letter to the new Minister requesting that he move us to the tower near the Victory Palace Hotel and move the cabinet members into the *open space* where we currently worked.

Addressing my colleagues, I said, "This is a democratic decision that will require everyone to vote. Those who are in agreement with the petition raise your hand."

There was silence. I asked the question again, but not one hand was raised. Everyone bowed their heads.

Just when I thought everyone was against my petition, I saw one hand go up at the back of the room. It was the hand of a young woman. Small in stature, hair braided and pulled back, she was wearing a pink uniform. It was Pauline Moukila, the woman responsible for maintenance of the office and building. I looked at her for a few seconds and told her in front of everyone: "Miss, I admire your courage as much as I am disappointed by the cowardice of my colleagues. But I am sorry, I cannot write this letter. We will continue to work in this open space since that appears to be everyone's preference...."

In the days that followed, I inquired about Pauline Moukila. She had obtained her bachelor's degree in Commercial Management and could not continue her studies because she was raising her two children alone.

I summoned her to my desk and told her, "Miss Moukila, I have decided to send you to Paris for six months to receive training in personal management from the Suez Group. Everything in France will be taken care of, including the care of your children. When you return, you will become my assistant."

As she was leaving my area with tears in her eyes, I thought to myself that I had probably just made the most important hire of my entire career.

Chapter 11

MY FATHER'S OFFICE, JOHN STREET, NEW YORK CITY 1953
-
Billy Collins

He would take me with him when I was a boy
before that was something people did,
the two of us riding the subway,
then walking a few blocks in those canyon-like streets
to the insurance company where he worked.

There, he would set me free to wander
up and down the long rows of typists,
clacking away on their manual machines,
fingernails red and hands blue
from the carbon paper, famous
for working the miracle of the triplicate.

The place was an Avalon of supplies—
reams of paper, envelopes neat in their boxes,
even a franking machine, your own private post office.

Sometimes I would stop to look down
on the wide expanse of New York Harbor
never guessing how many of the office's
rituals and devices would soon disappear for good
into the gaping maw of obsolescence.

Now the oasis of the water cooler is gone,
and silenced is the aggregate racket of typing.

Blown away is the haze of smoke from cigarettes.
Gone, the ashtrays from every desk
and the bigger ones by the elevators,
their sand kept smooth and clean
as if tended every night by a tiny man with a rake.

No more thick tear-off calendars,
the days disappearing one page at a time.

No more fountain pen drawing
its nectar from the black flower of an ink bottle.

No more black rotary phone,
ringing with good news, bad news, and worse.

Gone, the switchboard and the intercom,
cable room, Rolodex, and Dictaphone.

Gone, too, the many paperweights
that weighed down the stacks of papers
keeping them from blowing way
on a hot summer day with the windows wide open
and tall fans oscillating this way and that,
and men in shirtsleeves leaning
out high windows to catch a breeze.

Goodbye to the hat rack and the hats they held,
and gone the men themselves and gone my father,
gone my father as well.

Farewell, too, to the adding machine
and the spindle where memos were impaled.
They went away while you were out.

But stay, oh paperclip
and stay, oh rubber band
still keepers of order, logic, and sense

from the days of saloons and nightsticks,
evening editions and newsreels

to this day when you two wait at the ready
in the cubicle of a worker
in a towering glassy building,

she who is looking at a screen
as she uses a mouse to download an elephant,
of all things, and print out its picture in color,
the huge creature traveling through a wire,
then three of them materializing in her hand, a miracle in triplicate.

ABOUT THE CONTRIBUTORS

JONATHAN AMES is the author of the novels *You Were Never Really Here* (recently adapted into a film starring Joaquin Phoenix), *Wake Up, Sir!*, *The Extra Man*, and *I Pass Like Night*; a graphic novel, *The Alcoholic* (with artwork by Dean Haspiel); and the essay collections *The Double Life Is Twice as Good*, *I Love You More Than You Know*, *My Less Than Secret Life*, and *What's Not to Love?*. He is the editor of *Sexual Metamorphosis: An Anthology of Transsexual Memoirs* and the winner of a Guggenheim Fellowship. He is also the creator of the TV series *Bored to Death* (HBO) and *Blunt Talk* (Starz).

LEE CHILD is the author of 22 Jack Reacher novels, which have sold more than 100 million copies and been translated into 47 languages. Two of the Reacher series, *One Shot* and *Never Go Back*, were adapted into blockbuster films. Prior to his writing career, he worked at Granada Television. Fired in 1995 at the age of 40 as a result of corporate restructuring, he saw an opportunity where others might have seen a crisis. Always a voracious reader, he bought six dollars' worth of paper and pencils and sat down to write a book. That book was *Killing Floor*, the first in the Jack Reacher series. *The Midnight Line*, the 23rd Jack Reacher novel, comes out in November 2017.

BILLY COLLINS is the author of 12 collections of poetry, including *The Rain in Portugal*, *Aimless Love*, *Horoscopes for the Dead*, *Ballistics*, and *The Trouble with Poetry*. A former US Poet Laureate (2001 to 2003) and New York State Poet (2004 to 2006), he is also the editor of *Poetry 180: A Turning Back to Poetry, 180 More: Extraordinary Poems for Every Day* and *Bright Wings: An Illustrated Anthology of Poems About Birds*. He is a former Distinguished Professor of English at Lehman College and Senior Distinguished Fellow at the Winter Park Institute at Rollins College. In 2016, he was inducted into the American Academy of Arts and Letters.

SLOANE CROSLEY is the author of the essay collections *I Was Told There'd Be Cake* and *How Did You Get This Number* and the novel *The Clasp*. She is a contributing editor at *Vanity Fair* and *Interview* magazines and has contributed to a variety of anthologies, including *The 50 Funniest American Writers: An Anthology of Humor from Mark Twain to The Onion*. Her new book of essays, *Look Alive Out There*, will be published in April 2018 by Farrar, Straus and Giroux.

JOSHUA FERRIS is the author of the novels *Then We Came to the End*, *The Unnamed*, and *To Rise Again at a Decent Hour* and the short-story collection *The Dinner Party*. He is the winner of the Barnes & Noble Discover Award, the PEN/Hemingway Award and the International Dylan Thomas Prize.

JONATHAN SAFRAN FOER is the author of the novels *Everything Is Illuminated*, for which he won the Guardian First Book Prize, the National Jewish Book Award and the New York Public Library Young Lions Prize; *Extremely Loud & Incredibly Close*; and *Here I Am*. His works of nonfiction are *Eating Animals* and *New American Haggadah*. He adapted the work of Bruno Schulz for the art book *Tree of Codes*. He teaches creative writing at NYU.

ROXANE GAY is the author of the novel *An Untamed State*, the story collections *Ayiti* and *Difficult Women*, the collection of essays *Bad Feminist* and the memoir *Hunger*. She wrote *Black Panther: World of Wakanda* for Marvel Comics and is a contributing opinion writer for *The New York Times*. She is an associate professor of English at Purdue University.

CHIP KIDD is a writer and graphic designer. He is associate art director at Alfred A. Knopf (where he has worked since 1986) and editor at large for Pantheon graphic novels. He is the author of two novels, *The Cheese Monkeys* and *The Learners*, and the original graphic novel *Batman: Death by Design*, and he has designed over 2,000 book jackets. He has been honored with the A.I.G.A. Medal, the National Design Award and the Infinity Award from the International Center of Photography. *Chip Kidd: Book Two: Work 2007-2017* will be published in fall 2017 by Rizzoli.

VALERIA LUISELLI is the author of the novels *The Story of My Teeth* and *Faces in the Crowd*, for which she won the *Los Angeles Times* Art Seidenbaum Award and the National Book Foundation's "5 Under 35" Award, and the essay collections *Sidewalks* and *Tell Me How It Ends*. Her new novel, *The Lost Children Archives*, is forthcoming from Alfred A. Knopf.

ALAIN MABANCKOU is a novelist, poet and professor of literature at UCLA. His books published in English translation include *African Psycho, Blue White Red, Broken Glass, Black Bazaar, Tomorrow I'll Be Twenty, The Lights of Pointe-Noire,* and *Black Moses*. He was awarded the Renaudot Prize in 2006 and has been nominated twice for the Man Booker International Prize.

AIMEE MANN is an award-winning singer-songwriter whose latest album, *Mental Illness*, was released in 2017. Her other solo albums include *Charmer, @#%&*! Smilers, One More Drifter in the Snow,* and *The Forgotten Arm.* Her song "Save Me," part of the original music she contributed to the *Magnolia* soundtrack, earned both Academy Award and Grammy Award nominations. NPR has named her one of the "Top 10 Best Living Songwriters." **JONATHAN COULTON** is a singer-songwriter whose latest album, *Solid State*, was released in 2017. His eight albums include his 2003 debut, *Smoking Monkey*, and *Artificial Heart*, which reached the Billboard charts. He is currently the one-man house band for the NPR quiz show *Ask Me Another*.

JOYCE CAROL OATES is the author of more than 70 books, including novels, short-story collections, poetry, plays, essays and criticism, among them *Where Are You Going, Where Have You Been?, We Were the Mulvaneys, Blonde, The Lost Landscape: A Writer's Coming of Age,* and *A Book of American Martyrs.* Among her many honors are the National Humanities Medal, the PEN/ Malamud Award for Excellence in Short Fiction, the National Book Award, and membership in the American Academy of Arts and Letters. She is the Roger S. Berlind '52 Distinguished Professor of the Humanities (Emeritus) at Princeton University.

GARY SHTEYNGART is the author of the memoir *Little Failure* and the novels *Super Sad True Love Story*, for which he won the Bollinger Everyman Wodehouse Prize; *Absurdistan*; and *The Russian Debutante's Handbook*, for which he won the Stephen Crane Award for First Fiction and the National Jewish Book Award for Fiction. He teaches at Columbia University.

ABOUT

Speaking of Work is the result of an extraordinary collaboration. Through Project: SET THE PAGE FREE, fourteen storytellers of different perspectives, geographies and genres worked together to create a multi-faceted, multi-lensed portrait of the workplace today. Behind the scenes, behind the pages, Xerox® technology and innovations helped enable the work, the collaboration and sharing of ideas.

Xerox® technology, software and apps employed in the creation of the book:

ConnectKey® Technology and the VersaLink® C405 Multifunction Printer enabled secure collaboration and communication across countries and continents, with enhanced productivity and security. DocuShare® Flex made content collaboration effortless. Easy Translator Service translated content around the world at the touch of a button. Xerox Apps for Google Drive & Dropbox empowered digital sharing through the cloud. Print Authentication provided device security using a smart phone. Voice Recognition Technology made productivity as simple as speaking. @PrintbyXerox App enabled printing from virtually anywhere. XMPie® software made the eBook personalized for each recipient. And the printed book was produced on an iGen4 ® Press and Xerox Nuvera® 144 EA Production System using a FreeFlow® Print Server.

THE CAUSE

Xerox supports global literacy through the making of this book, benefiting literacy outreach programs of the 92nd Street Y and Worldreader. For more than 140 years, the 92nd Street Y has put literature into the community, brought the world's great writers to the stage and shared their work with readers across the globe. Worldreader's mission is to create a world where everyone can be a reader, promoting global literacy through e-readers and digital libraries in underserved communities in over 50 countries.